Dancing
on the Inside

Glen C. Strathy

iUniverse, Inc.
Bloomington

Dancing on the Inside

iUniverse books may be ordered through booksellers or by contacting:

iUniverse
1663 Liberty Drive
Bloomington, IN 47403
www.iuniverse.com
1-800-Authors (1-800-288-4677)

ISBN: 978-1-4620-1871-0 (sc)
ISBN: 978-1-4620-1870-3 (hc)
ISBN: 978-1-4620-1869-7 (e)

Printed in the United States of America

iUniverse rev. date: 06/20/2011

For the real Jenny.

"Dance as though no one is watching."

Acknowledgements

Many thanks to the students and staff of the Kingston School of Dance, who bear absolutely no resemblance to characters in this book but who provided the atmosphere in which the idea for it was born. Thanks as well to Brian Henry for providing valuable comments and encouragement.

Chapter 1

Dance School

"You know, it's not too late to back out," Jenny's mother said over the squeak of the windshield wipers and the drumming of rain on the car roof.

It was the twentieth time that morning Jenny had heard these words. She turned her head to stare out the rain-splattered window beside her. Between the clouds and the damp asphalt, the streets looked even greyer than usual. "I know," she said.

"If you decide after today you don't like it, I can get a refund. But if you go to two classes and then change your mind, I can't get the money back."

"I know," said Jenny. They were driving through an older part of town, with tall trees and sidewalks. The houses were big, with peeling paint and weedy gardens, but Jenny liked them because they were all different. Some had second-floor balconies and round, tower-like rooms on the corners. Some had wrap-around porches and gingerbread trim. There was a stone house that looked like a miniature castle and another that looked like it belonged to some

Goth family. *If only someone would fix them up,* Jenny thought. *They're so beautiful.*

"And I can probably return the clothes too, except for the tights."

Jenny glared at the back of her mother's head. "Mom! I want to do it. You promised."

Glancing up at the rearview mirror, her mother's eyes met Jenny's. "I'm sorry, honey," she said. "I'm sure you'll have fun. And make lots of friends. Well, I hope so, anyway. And if not, there's always that Girl Guides chapter I saw advertised."

Jenny growled her annoyance. "I'm too old for Guides. It's called Pathfinders once you're twelve. And besides, I don't want to do it."

A few minutes later, her mother turned the car into a small parking lot and stopped. "Well, this is the address," she said. She peered at the long stone building next to them. "Looks a bit run down to me. But maybe it's newer on the inside. The website said the studio was fully equipped."

Jenny got out of the car and pulled her raincoat tight over her white leotard and tights. She had chosen white because she thought it looked like what dancers would wear. Jenny had put on this outfit the night before and slept in it, hoping it would make her feel more like a dancer herself. But the cool September air made her shiver a little.

They walked up the rusty metal steps, through the heavy front door, and down the corridor. There were lots of closed doors along the way, leading to little offices that were shut on Saturday. Some looked as though they'd been shut for a long time. At the end, one door stood open next to a sign that read "Kingston Ballet School."

Jenny felt her stomach tighten as they went inside. This was her first time inside a real dance school, and she had no idea what to expect.

She had seen one ballet in her life. Two years ago, her grandparents had sent her a DVD of *Swan Lake* for Christmas. It was an old Russian production. Jenny had set it aside, unopened, for almost a year. Then one day after school, curiosity and boredom inspired her to watch it, and it awoke in her a fascination that was both surprising and irresistible.

Jenny had watched *Swan Lake* hundreds of times since then, often pausing it so she could draw pictures of the dancers in different poses, leaping through the air, gliding across the floor, twirling. Her parents eventually bought her a portable DVD player so they wouldn't have to see the same performance over and over on the big TV. The more she studied *Swan Lake*, the more Jenny longed to be part of the world she saw on the screen, a world of astounding beauty. But she had never seen live ballet or met a dancer in person.

The room was lined with shabby beige couches. A pile of brochures sat on a badly scratched coffee table. Bits and pieces of scenery leaned against one wall, next to what looked like a box of old junk. On another wall hung a pink Bristol board sign saying "Volunteers Needed!" with a sign-up sheet stapled underneath. At the far end, a large table and chairs had been set up. No one else was there.

Jenny's mother started to help her take her coat off, but Jenny pulled away and did it herself. They were just about to sit down when a woman strode in from a doorway on the other side of the big table.

She had short, brown hair and a round body. Beige-rimmed eyeglasses hung from a string around her neck, overtop a pink sweater.

At first glance, Jenny thought she looked more like a librarian than a dancer. Only her black tights and ballet slippers said anything different. "Hello!" she said, smiling.

Jenny's mother walked over to the woman. "Hi. I'm Marilyn Spark. This is my daughter, Jenny. I phoned the other day."

"Yes, of course," said the woman, in a slight French accent. "You're a bit early. But that's good. Most of the other students have already registered." She turned to Jenny. "Hello, Jenny. You may call me Madame Beaufort. I'll be one of your teachers."

Jenny gave her a slight smile but said nothing. Madame Beaufort looked down at Jenny's feet and frowned slightly. "It's still raining, isn't it?"

"Yes," said Jenny.

"Well, from now on, please don't wear your ballet slippers outside. It's not good for the slippers, and it gets them dirty. We have a room just down the hall where you can change into your dance outfit right before class."

Jenny's mother glanced quickly at Jenny's feet. "You changed shoes in the car!" she exclaimed.

Jenny nodded.

Madame Beaufort looked Jenny up and down and then turned back to her mother. "It's fine for today, but for the next class, she'll need a black leotard. A black silhouette against a white wall helps us see whether a student is standing correctly. Also, she will need pink tights. That's 'ballet pink,' not regular pink. We like it if all the girls dress the same."

Jenny began twisting a lock of her hair around her index finger.

"She'll also need to come with her hair arranged up off her neck, preferably in a bun at the back. And she'll need to let her bangs grow out from now on. Can't dance with hair in her eyes."

"I see," her mother replied.

Madame Beaufort looked at Jenny again. "First time taking dance?"

"Yes," Jenny said. The knot in her stomach was getting bigger. The class hadn't even started, and already she'd messed up.

"Well, it won't take you too long to catch up."

"This is a beginners' class, isn't it?" her mother asked, a little concerned.

"This is Grade Four Ballet, for twelve-year-olds," Madame Beaufort explained. "Most of the girls are returning students. But don't worry. Everyone must start somewhere. She can work at her own pace for now. I think you'll be amazed at how quickly her strength and flexibility will improve." She looked down at Jenny again. "Not to mention posture and poise."

Jenny tried to stand a little straighter. The lock of her hair was now very tight.

Madame Beaufort sat down behind the table and opened up a file folder. "Now, I'll need you to fill in a registration form." She smiled at Jenny. "You can go on down the hall and see the studio if you like, while we get you registered."

"Okay," said Jenny. Her stomach was getting tighter by the minute. Jenny had hoped the other students would be beginners too. Now she knew that she would be the worst dancer in the class. And it hadn't even started yet!

But she was curious to see the studio.

Madame Beaufort pointed to the archway behind the table. "It's just down the hall. The first two doors are the changing rooms.

You can hang up your raincoat in the girls'. The studio is at the far end."

"Have fun, honey," said her mother. "Do you want me to wait around, just in case? Or should I just pick you up after?" She stroked Jenny's back reassuringly with one hand.

"After," said Jenny. And she started cautiously down the hall.

The wall on the left was covered with framed photographs. Each photo showed a group of children, almost all girls, in a frozen tableau from some past performance. Some were dressed as clowns, pirates, or animals. Others wore abstract costumes that reminded Jenny of rainbows or fairies. None of them wore white, puffy skirts like in *Swan Lake*. But they were all dancing ballet. The girls looked so strong and graceful. They were obviously having fun. Jenny felt a deep pang of envy and longing combined.

In the girls' changing room, Jenny hung her raincoat on a hook and then checked the bottom of her slippers. They were a little damp but not too dirty. She wished she had chosen a black leotard rather than white. The last thing she wanted was to stand out.

Then she went to look for the studio.

The studio floor was a few inches higher than the hall floor and had a slightly springy feel to it. It was a big, empty room with white walls and a high ceiling. Full-length mirrors and wooden rails ran along one wall. A piano stood in one corner, covered by a quilted cloth. A stereo system sat on a small shelf unit.

Jenny felt very small as she walked to the centre of the room. *So this is where real dancers practise and learn,* she thought.

The more she looked around, the more Jenny found herself wondering if she really belonged here. With each passing moment, she felt sure she didn't. The girls in the photographs all looked so happy and confident. Jenny had nothing in common with them. She didn't feel confident at all. She felt like a trespasser.

Jenny didn't want to wait for the girls in the photographs to arrive. She didn't belong with them. They would stare at her wrong-coloured leotard and her long hair and know she was not a dancer. She wished she were at home, curled up in her room with a sketch pad. Maybe there was still time to leave before anyone else saw her. Maybe she should tell her mother to ask for a refund. She hoped she wouldn't be too annoyed.

Jenny was just turning to leave when she heard the sounds of light, hurried footsteps coming from down the hall. Too late. The other students were coming. Jenny held her breath. Her feet froze to the floor, and she paused, waiting for them to burst into the studio.

Chapter 2
No Way Out

Jenny heard a door swing, and the footsteps quieted. She guessed the newcomers had run into the changing room. Jenny didn't know what to do, so she stayed still, listening intently. She could hear the muffled voices of girls chatting to each other, the dull thuds of things being dropped on the floor, and the rustling of cloth. As minutes passed, the noises grew louder. Other people were arriving. Then the door creaked again, and the footsteps began growing louder, coming closer to the studio.

Jenny scanned the room. Not knowing what else to do, she ran over to the piano. She lifted the quilted cloth and peeked underneath. There was just enough room. Jenny ducked under the piano, under the cover, and out of sight. She sat down on the floor, knees in front of her chest, head down, peering through a gap in the fabric, hoping she was safely inconspicuous.

A few seconds later, three girls about Jenny's age walked into the studio. All of them wore black leotards over pink tights.

One girl, with auburn hair past her shoulders and a pimply face, was speaking. "So, Veronique, did you do that workshop over the summer?"

"You can't just do it," Veronique replied. She was tall, with blonde hair tightly held in a bun and a slightly regal look about her. "You have to pass the audition first. Plus, you usually have to go to one of the best schools already before they'll let you in. But I might try out for next summer's workshop."

"You should, you know. You're really good."

"Maybe we all should," said the third girl. She was skinny, with a dark complexion, and her tights had small holes on both knees. Her hair was arranged in two black pigtails, placed lopsidedly on the back of her head.

"Oh, I don't think they'd take me," said the pimply-faced girl.

"Why not, Trish? You had fun in last year's show, didn't you?"

But before Trish could reply, the girl with the pigtails continued. "Hey, do you think we're going to learn to go on point this year?"

Veronique looked disapprovingly at her. "It's not 'on point.' It's '*en pointe.*'" She made the second word sound like "pwahnt."

"Well, whatever. I just want to try dancing on my toes." And with that she began to dance a circle around her friends, stepping on the balls of her feet.

As she twisted another lock of hair, Jenny watched the girl closely. She was not as graceful as the dancers Jenny had seen before, but she looked like she was enjoying herself and had obviously danced before.

"My mother says we might start pointe work next term," said Veronique. "But you need to practise more. Look, it's like this." She repeated the other girl's steps but with a little more poise and precision.

"Yeah, well, it's been a while." And the pigtailed girl did the dance over again, nearly the same as before.

"Hi, Veronique. Hi, Trish. Hi, Ara," said a voice from the hall.

A fourth girl ran into the studio. She was dressed like the others and had thick, curly, brown hair tied in a loose ponytail.

"Hi, Kristen," said Ara and Veronique.

Kristen looked at Trish. "Oh, good. We don't have to have our hair up today."

"We're supposed to," said Veronique.

Trish looked blankly at Veronique for a second and then gasped, putting her hands up to her head. "I forgot!"

"Well, at least I won't be the only one," said Kristen. "My hair grew so much over the summer that when I tried to put it in a bun, it came out so big it looked like I had a coconut on my head. I need to get it cut or straightened or something for next week."

All four girls laughed. For a second, Jenny smiled too. Then Ara, the girl with pigtails, turned her head, and her eyes met Jenny's through the gap in the fabric for the first time. Jenny's stomach flipped over. She dropped her head, squeezed her eyes shut, and hugged her knees a little tighter. She wished she could turn invisible.

Seconds later, Jenny felt a slight change in the air. She opened her eyes and found Ara squatting in front of her, holding back the piano cover. "Hey, look, guys!" Ara shouted over her shoulder. "There's someone under here." Turning to Jenny, she demanded, "Who are you?"

Just then, Madame Beaufort strode briskly into the studio, followed by two other girls and a boy dressed in black tights and a white T-shirt. He was wearing ballet slippers too—black ones. Ara stood up, still holding back the cover, leaving Jenny exposed.

Everyone looked at her curiously except for the boy, who immediately chose a spot on the railing away from the girls and draped his arms over it, as though trying to look cool.

"Good morning, girls," said Madame Beaufort. "Gather 'round, please."

The rest of the class followed the instruction at once. But Jenny just hugged her legs even tighter. She felt light-headed and dizzy. There was a high-pitched buzzing in her ears.

Madame Beaufort had obviously noticed Jenny sitting by herself and called out, "Jenny, would you please join us."

Jenny said nothing. She didn't look up. Two seconds later, she heard footsteps approaching. She opened her eyes. This time, Jenny found herself looking up at Madame Beaufort.

"Please come and join us," said Madame Beaufort.

In a small, panicky whisper, Jenny replied, "I can't."

Madame Beaufort looked into Jenny's eyes and seemed to recognize that something was seriously the matter. She squatted down and whispered, "What's wrong, Jenny?"

Jenny couldn't explain. She wasn't entirely sure herself. All she knew was that she couldn't budge from her spot—and that she wished she could make herself disappear. "Please," she said, "can I just sit here for a while?"

"Are you not feeling well?" Madame Beaufort asked kindly. "Your mother might still be in the lounge. If she is, would you like me to get her?"

"No," Jenny said at once. The last thing she wanted was more attention. "Please, can I just sit here and watch? I won't make a sound. Can I?"

Madame Beaufort looked concerned but also a bit uncertain.

She seemed to be weighing the situation in her mind. She put a hand momentarily on Jenny's forehead. "Do you feel like you're going to be sick?" she asked.

"Yes. I mean, no," said Jenny. "I'll be okay if I just sit for a while."

"All right," Madame Beaufort decided. "But let me know if it gets worse."

"I will," Jenny whispered.

All the other girls were now looking at Jenny with curious expressions on their faces. Jenny hung her head again to avoid their eyes.

Madame Beaufort stood up, crossed the room, and stood in the circle with the others. She quickly took attendance. Then she smiled and said, "Well, welcome back, everyone. It's nice to be together again. You'll be learning lots of new things this year, and not just from me. We have a new teacher who will be working with you on Mondays. Her name is Katrina Miles. She is a former soloist with the National Ballet Company, so I expect you'll be able to learn a lot from her."

The students smiled and exchanged glances at this news.

"However, right now, you need to begin getting your muscles back in shape after your summer holiday. So let's start with our warm-up."

Jenny watched intently as Madame Beaufort led the girls through a series of stretches: pointing and flexing their toes, leaning forward toward their outstretched feet and then to each side, putting the soles of their feet together and gently pushing their knees to the floor.

Watching from her spot under the piano, Jenny was fascinated with everything the class did. She tried to memorize each exercise.

She made a list in her head and ran over it as she watched. She still hugged her legs tightly. But now that no one was watching her, she no longer felt dizzy, just frozen.

Madame Beaufort had the girls stand up and take a spot along the railing, which she called the *barre*.

"I'm afraid we've lost our pianist this term," Madame Beaufort explained as she turned on the sound system.

Although all the students seemed to know what to do, Madame Beaufort checked their posture in various positions. They had to bend and straighten their knees. *Demi-pliés*, Madame Beaufort called the exercise. These were followed by *relevés*, *retirés*, and *battement tendus*.

The class progressed from the barre to slow exercises in the middle of the floor, to fast steps that took them across the floor. Jenny couldn't keep up with all the names for these movements. But as she watched, she compared them with her memory of *Swan Lake*. The students in this class were a lot younger and only just learning. But Jenny could see similarities. It was as if each exercise Madame Beaufort presented—each stance, each movement—was a letter of an alphabet. Each one waiting to be used in a word that would make up a sentence. *If only you knew how to write with that alphabet,* Jenny thought, *could you make* Swan Lake *appear? Or could you create a new ballet all your own?*

Even though all the girls tried to execute the movements perfectly, with Madame Beaufort's encouragement, Jenny became fascinated with how each student's personality came through in her—or his—dancing.

Veronique, with her head held high and her back straight, looked composed and confident. Yet her movements seemed a little stiff, and her face, still as a statue, seemed so serious.

Trish, on the other hand, kept stealing glances in the mirror, looking to see whether she had the movements and positions right. Whenever she made a mistake, she would stop and start again.

And then there was Ara, who seemed to throw herself into each move, always looking slightly off balance. Her face glowed with enthusiasm, as though each exercise was a roller-coaster ride taking her to a new and surprising destination.

Only one other student looked as though she might be as much of a beginner as Jenny—a girl named Robyn, whose red hair was arranged in a bun as tight as Veronique's. Robyn certainly had no fear of participating in the class, the way Jenny did. Yet she looked like she wasn't quite sure she wanted to be there. At times, she seemed to be fighting her own instincts—trying to copy the movements but always starting with the wrong foot or the wrong arm—constantly looking around at the other girls to check what they were doing.

As the class progressed, Jenny lost all sense of time. The experience was magical, like watching *Swan Lake*, only less predictable. And while *Swan Lake* was a dream world, the ballet class was real. These girls were near Jenny's age. They had voices. She could hear the thud of each footstep and feel the vibrations in the floor when the students moved in unison. There was no separation. And Jenny was overjoyed by that fact, and also terrified.

When class ended, Jenny dashed out ahead of the other girls, making sure no one, not even Madame Beaufort, had a chance to speak to her. She grabbed her raincoat from the change room and elbowed her way through the waiting room where a crowd of parents and students were gathering for the next class.

Jenny's mother was just coming in the front door of the building, carrying the running shoes Jenny had left in the car. Jenny whipped off her slippers, grabbed the shoes, stuck her feet in them, and led the way out the door.

Once they had buckled their seat belts, her mother glanced at Jenny through the rearview mirror and asked, "So, how was it?"

"Great," Jenny lied. She knew that if she told her mother the truth, she wouldn't be allowed to go to the next dance class. And she knew, as deeply as she had ever known anything, that she had to go back.

Chapter 3

A Bold Plan

The rain had stopped and the sky had turned a lighter shade of grey, but Jenny hardly noticed as her mother started the car and pulled out of the parking lot. She slunk down in her seat, her mind full of what had just happened. She had been in a real ballet class. She had discovered a few precious secrets about how dancers train. And she couldn't wait to write them down.

The car came to a stop in the driveway of the Sparks' new home. It was a modest, yellow-brick house, old enough to have gone through more than one set of previous owners. Jenny jumped out and ran to the door. Feeling impatient, she tried the handle and rang the bell. But then her mother caught up with her and unlocked the door with a key.

Jenny dashed through the door and pried off her shoes. "Hi, Dad!" she yelled in the direction of the living room, where her father was unpacking books. Then she ran up the stairs to her new room.

The family had only moved into this house two days before, and everything was still in chaos. The floor of Jenny's room was completely covered in half-unpacked cardboard boxes and their former contents. Only the bed was in its proper place.

Jenny hunted through boxes until she found a pen and one of the notebooks her mother had bought her for school. Then she went down the hall to the room that was destined to be her father's office. This was the emptiest room in the house at the moment, containing only a desk, a chair, a file cabinet, and a stack of book boxes in a corner.

Jenny closed the door and sat on the floor, her back against the wall. Quickly, she began jotting down the exercises she had watched in ballet class. But after a few minutes, she realized it was no good. There were too many details. Already some of the finer points were fading from her memory.

Then, just before she put the pen down, Jenny had an idea. She was alone in the room, still wearing her leotard and tights. Both her parents were downstairs. Perhaps she could try actually doing some of the exercises.

Jenny took a deep breath to steady herself. She put her notebook aside and slid over so that her back was against the door. She didn't want anyone bursting in on her unexpectedly. She sat up straight, legs together in front of her.

The first thing the class had done was to alternately point and flex their toes. Jenny slowly tried it. It seemed simple enough. Next, she slid her hands down her legs, bending forward at the same time as far as she could. She was disappointed to discover that she couldn't reach her toes, as the girls in class had. Trying to stretch beyond a certain point produced a sharp pain at the back of her knees. But, as Madame Beaufort had said, perhaps she would grow more flexible with practice.

Jenny sat up, opened her legs in a V, and repeated the stretch on each leg separately. She felt a delicious pleasure in knowing that she was taking a tiny, secretive step toward being a dancer.

Doing the exercises made her remember a few more details, so she recorded these in her notebook, adding little drawings for clarity.

The next thing the class had reviewed were positions. Jenny stood up and tried to assume the first position from memory—heels together, toes apart so her feet made a V. She couldn't turn her feet out as far as the other girls could, either. But she didn't want to push herself, not the first time anyway. She put her hands down in front of her, palms up, with her arms slightly rounded—the beginning position, or *bras bas*, as Madame Beaufort had called it. Then she raised her arms in front of her, as if she were holding a huge beach ball. That was the first position.

Struggling to remember exactly what she had seen in class, she moved her right foot to the side so that her heels were apart and spread her arms wider to make second position. For third position, she drew her right heel in front of and touching the arch of her left foot—arms down, right arm farther out than the left.

Jenny wanted to look in a mirror to see if she was doing it right. But there was no full-length mirror in the office, and the one for her room hadn't been unpacked yet.

So Jenny picked up her notebook and walked across the hall to the bathroom. The mirror over the sink was too high. But by standing on the edge of the bathtub, she could see most of her body.

Jenny put her arms in *bras bas* again. The part she could see looked okay. Then she moved her arms into first position. Also fine.

She wanted to check whether she was standing with her back straight, as the other girls had done. But turning sideways on the narrow tub ledge was impossible. Her back felt straight, anyway.

Jenny hopped down and added drawings of the first three positions to her notebook.

For the next part, she needed a barre. The towel bar might do, but it was too high. *Perhaps,* Jenny thought, *the last people who had lived here didn't have children.*

Then Jenny had an idea. She put the toilet lid down and climbed on top of it. Reaching out with one arm, she rested her fingers on the towel bar, which was now the right height. She put her feet and her free hand in first position, bent her knees into a *demi-plié,* and then straightened them.

Then, for fun, she slid one foot out to the side, toe pointed, like the *battement tendus* she had seen the other students do.

"Hey, that looks good," came a sudden voice from the hall.

Startled, Jenny turned sharply and saw her father standing in the doorway. As she did so, her foot slipped out from under her. She clutched the towel bar for support, but the weight of her falling body pulled the screws holding the bar out of the wall.

Jenny's bottom hit the edge of toilet seat, and then she slid off backward. Her back hit the wall, and she came to rest with her legs across the toilet seat, her body wedged between the toilet and the wall, and her left arm on the floor, holding the towel bar.

Jenny wasn't really hurt, but the shock made her pause for a second.

Her father hurried over and helped her get to her feet. "Sorry," he said. "Maybe I spoke too soon. Are you okay? Nothing broken?"

"Just this," said Jenny, holding up the towel bar. They both looked at it and laughed.

"Well, we can fix that," said her father, taking the bar from her. "But I thought you were taking ballet dancing, not toilet seat dancing."

Jenny felt her face flush. "I am. I mean, I'm not. I mean ... I'm sorry."

He laughed. "It's all right. But maybe you should save dancing for class. You looked like a scene from *Vertigo*."

"What's *Vertigo*?" asked Jenny.

"Oh, just an old movie about a man who had to quit work because he got dizzy every time he stood on a chair." Her father sat on the edge of the tub. "Anyway, I guess you must have enjoyed your first dance class."

"I did," said Jenny, a little hesitantly. "Well, I loved watching anyway."

Her father gave Jenny an encouraging look. "So what do you think? Would you like to be a ballerina?"

"Oh, yes, I'd love it," Jenny said, her eyes widening, heart leaping.

"Wow." Her father smiled. "That must have been some class."

"It wasn't just today," Jenny explained. "You know I've been dreaming of it for months. Today just made it more real."

"Well, I'm glad. You know your mother really wants you to start making new friends here. Dance classes are a great place to begin."

Jenny's face fell. For the first time since coming home, she thought of the fear that had gripped her in class. She began to twist a lock of her hair. "Thing is, though, I'm not sure I can do it. I'm not sure I can dance like the others."

"But you'd like to?"

Jenny nodded.

"Well, just give yourself a chance. Find out if it's as much fun as you expect. If you want to do it, you'll find a way."

Jenny liked it when her father said things like this. Somehow, his honest faith in her made her worries subside. She could feel her body relax a little. She let go of her lock of hair.

Her father stood up. "Well, I just came to tell you lunch is ready. And also to ask if you'd like to help me unpack a few boxes this afternoon. Some of your things are waiting to be brought upstairs."

"Sure," Jenny answered with enthusiasm. "Just give me two minutes."

After her father left, Jenny wrote everything else she could remember from class in her notebook. Then she crossed the hall to her room, rummaged through a cardboard box for a T-shirt and jeans, changed into them, and went downstairs.

After lunch, Jenny asked her mother to show her how to put her long, dirty-blonde hair into a bun. It took Jenny several tries to get it tight enough to stay in place. Then she talked her mother into making a trip to the dance supply store to exchange her white leotard for a black one.

That night, just before bed, Jenny snuck into her father's office and did the ballet exercises again, as well as she could remember, anyway. She was just going back to her room when she heard her mother's voice drifting up the stairs.

"… just wish she had picked something other than ballet, something that didn't involve performing."

Jenny tiptoed to the top of the stairs where she could hear better.

"Why not, if it's something she's interested in?" her father replied.

"I just don't want her to go through the same kind of thing I did. I don't want her to get so hooked on ballet that she decides to become a dancer. I've asked a few people. It's incredibly expensive to put a girl through ballet lessons. It takes years of training to become a professional. Most girls don't make it, and the ones who do usually have to retire before they reach thirty-five."

"And what if she doesn't make it?" her mother continued. "She's so smart. But could we afford to send her to university after that?"

Jenny hated listening when her mother got on this negative sort of rant. She would have gone back to her room, but she wanted to hear her father's reply.

"I think you're getting a little ahead of yourself," he said. "She may not want a career in ballet. Why not just look at this as a chance for her to make some friends?"

"I hope she does." Her mother sighed. "I worry that she's so shy. If she doesn't get over her problem soon, what will her teenage years be like? She's too much like me."

"That's not all bad," said her father.

"Oh, yes it is. And the stress of being in a new school won't help. That's why I wish she would join a group where they make a real effort to get the girls to socialize."

"We did promise her."

"Yes, for now. But if she doesn't make some friends, I think we'll have to look at other options."

Her father sighed. "Yes, I guess we will."

Jenny moved swiftly but quietly along the carpeted floor back to her room and bed. Her heart was pounding as she turned out the light and burrowed under the covers. They couldn't take her ballet away. Not so soon. It wasn't fair.

Her father had said that if she truly wanted something, she would find a way. And she wanted to be in that class. Okay, she would just have do so well and make so many friends that they'd have to let her continue.

And then Jenny thought again about the fear and paralysis that had gripped her in the studio. What if that happened again? What if it happened every time?

Her mother was right. Jenny had always been shy around people, maybe because she grew up outside the city, far from other relatives and neighbours. Her father had home-schooled her for the first three grades, and she still hadn't got the hang of regular school. She always seemed to be interested in different things than the other kids.

But this morning had been different. It was like her body and feelings had been trying to shut her down, to take her out of where she was. Could she bring herself to dance in class, in front of everyone? Even thinking about it made her stomach jitter and her legs and arms stiffen.

Yet, she so wanted be there. Just to be in that studio, just to watch, was wonderful in itself. To have permission to just sit, unnoticed, and take in everything—that would mean everything to her. She longed to see what new steps the girls would be learning, how much more there was to ballet that she couldn't yet imagine.

Of course, her mother wouldn't see it that way. She would see it as a waste of money if Jenny just sat and watched the class, if she remained a loner. And then there would be no more dance classes, ever again. *Besides,* Jenny thought, *Madame Beaufort probably wouldn't want a student who didn't dance.*

As Jenny was about to drift off to sleep, an idea came to her. Not a nice idea. A rather guilty idea, in fact. It was the kind of idea Jenny normally would have rejected without another thought. But this wasn't a normal occasion, and this idea seemed to offer her the only possible answer. It wouldn't work forever. And she might need to use her father's computer tomorrow to get some information from the Internet. But it might buy her some time. It would let her attend ballet classes for a while, maybe even long enough for her to find her own way, as her father would say.

Chapter 4

A Grande Deception

The following afternoon, Jenny began clearing out her room. She grabbed empty boxes from around the house and crammed them full of books, artwork, stuffed animals, and other things she and her mother had unpacked and arranged just two days earlier. Several bits of furniture had to go as well. It was hard for Jenny to part with her possessions. She had fond memories of them all. But she had a new purpose in life, and she needed floor space.

Just before dinner, Jenny heard her father trudge upstairs. There was a knock on the door, and when she opened it she found him balancing a box of books. The hallway leading to his office was completely blocked with Jenny's junk.

"What's all this?" her father asked, pointing to the clutter.

"Oh," said Jenny, "I decided I don't want any of that stuff in my new room. Could we just move it to the basement or get rid of it?"

Jenny's father set his box down and peered into a few of Jenny's. "Are you sure?" he said. "I thought you wanted these things?"

"I'm sure," Jenny replied. "I've decided I don't need them anymore."

He rolled his eyes. "Now you tell me."

"Sorry. I can help you move them if you like."

"We'll do it after dinner. What made you change your mind?"

"Oh, no reason. Just … new room, new house, new start."

In truth, Jenny had decided to do something she had never done before. She was going to lie to her parents. Not just a little white lie, but a big bold lie—a *Grande* Deception. She was going to make them think she was participating in dance class even though she wasn't.

The key to the plan, Jenny had decided, was to do everything to prevent suspicion. Nothing less would fool her mother. Jenny had never exercised much before. She hated gym at school. She found sports utterly boring. Now her body would have to change. She would have to start looking like a dancer—like someone who trained her body to perfection. And since she couldn't do it in class, she would practise at home, in the privacy of her room. Her room needed to become a miniature studio, without looking like a studio, of course. Everything she didn't absolutely need—everything that took up floor space—had to go. The only things she kept were her bed, her dresser, and a small desk for doing homework.

That night, before bed, Jenny repeated the exercises from ballet class one more time on her newly cleared floor.

On Monday after school, Jenny put her hair into a bun. This time, it took her only two tries. She stuffed her new black leotard, pink tights, and ballet slippers in her backpack so she could change into them at the ballet school. Then her father drove her to her second lesson.

Jenny had worked out a plan for when they arrived. When her

father stopped the car in the parking lot, Jenny said, "You don't have to come in with me. It's all right."

"Are you sure?" her father asked. "What if we have the time wrong?"

"Just let me look in the front door. If the school's open, I'll wave, and you can get a coffee at the donut shop or run an errand or something until the class ends." Jenny knew this would appeal to her father more than sitting in the waiting room.

"All right," he agreed.

Jenny jumped out of the car, ran up the steps, and pulled open the outside door. At the end of the corridor, the door to the dance school stood open as before. Jenny waved her father good-bye and went in.

Phase One successful, she thought. But that was the easy part.

Jenny hesitated. She knew what was waiting for her at the end of the hall, and she needed to breathe a few times before she was ready to face the journey.

Just then, Jenny heard the sound of the outside door being pulled open behind her. She turned her head quickly and saw Kristen standing in the door frame, looking back over her shoulder. Her mane of curly hair had been braided and fastened with a multicoloured scrunchie on the top of her head. "Hi!" she called to someone outside. A second later Trish joined her at the door, and the two girls entered the building.

Jenny turned her back to them and looked down at the floor as they passed her, chatting to each other. She waited until they were out of sight before setting off down the hall herself. As she approached the door to the school, Jenny hesitated. Her hand instinctively reached for a lock of hair to twist. But thanks to her bun, no loose hair was available—something else that would be different from now on.

Just as Jenny was about to step inside, a face framed by black pigtails popped around the edge of the door. Jenny found herself looking directly into Ara's brown eyes.

Jenny pulled her head back, as Ara's face lit up in surprise. "Oh," she said. "I thought you were going to be Lian."

Jenny's mouth opened, but she said nothing. Then Ara's eyes flashed with recognition. "Hey, you're the girl under the piano! Are you feeling better? What's your name?"

Ara grabbed Jenny's arm and pulled her inside. Jenny barely managed to sputter out her name when Ara began throwing a rush of words at her.

"I'm Ara. I'm glad you came back because I thought Saturday that you looked like you were more scared than sick. And I wanted to find out why and to tell you there's nothing to be nervous about even if it's your first time in ballet because you'll pick it up so easily. I've been taking ballet for four years now, and I love it. You brought your dance outfit, didn't you? Let me show you the change room, and you can meet everyone and get ready for class. There are always a few new people each year. What did you say your name was again?"

When they reached the girls' change room, Ara practically pushed Jenny inside. Most of the other girls from Saturday were there, in various stages of donning their dance wear and slippers.

"Look, everyone," Ara announced, "it's the girl under the piano. She came back after all."

Jenny was not sure she wanted to be known as "the girl under the piano." And now that she was here, she wasn't sure she liked the prospect of changing clothes in a room full of strangers. There were too many eyes staring at her. She could feel her body tensing, like it did when someone was about to take her picture. But she made herself choose a spot on one of the benches and unzip her bag. Ara plopped down next to her.

"Oh, great, another beginner." Jenny looked up. It was Veronique who had spoken.

"Shut up," said Robyn, who was sitting next to Veronique. "You're always so rude. I should tell Mom about it."

Veronique glared at Robyn as she pulled on her second slipper. "Yeah, and I should tell her you told me to shut up."

"Do it," said Robyn. "I need an excuse to practise my *chin na*."

Veronique drew herself up to her full height, picked up her dance bag, gave Robyn a condescending, "Puh," and walked out.

Robyn shook her head and started putting on her own slippers.

"Don't mind her," Ara said to Jenny. "She gets annoying sometimes. It's 'cause she thinks she's the best dancer in the school."

"She is the best dancer in the school," said Trish. "She always gets the lead role in the recitals."

Robyn hung her bag on a hook and marched out of the room.

Ara turned to Jenny. "Of course, it helps that their mom is Madame Beaufort."

"That's not the only reason," Kristen pointed out.

"Maybe not," Ara conceded. "But it's one reason."

Jenny changed out of her school clothes and into her dance outfit as quickly as possible. As she did, she deliberately avoided looking anyone in the eye, including Ara, who was busy changing herself.

Jenny noticed that Ara was wearing the same tights as last time. The holes in the knees had grown noticeably larger.

"You better tuck the ends of those strings inside," Ara commented as Jenny was tying on her slippers.

Just then, the door swung open. "Has anyone seen the new teacher?" asked the newcomer.

"Not yet," Kristen said.

Looking up, Jenny wasn't sure she recognized the girl who strode in. She had on a big, floppy wool hat, sunglasses, and a voluminous coat that completely concealed what she looked like underneath. "That's Lian," Ara whispered to Jenny.

"I looked her up on the Internet," Lian continued, as she began peeling off layers of clothing. "She was a soloist with the National Ballet for three years. And she studied at the National Ballet School before that. Plus, she did their teacher-training programme. I can't wait to meet her."

"I like Madame Beaufort," said Trish.

"Me, too," Lian said, "but this could be a great opportunity. Katrina Miles must know all kinds of important people—dancers, choreographers, theatre directors ... maybe even film producers."

"Are you hoping she'll make you into a star?" Kristen teased.

Lian ditched the last of her layers of street clothes and struck a pose. "Well, if she does, I'm ready."

Jenny was the last one to leave the change room. She lingered in the hallway, a notebook and pen in one hand, running over her plan in her mind. It was risky, but it was all she could think of.

Near the entrance to the waiting room, Madame Beaufort was talking with three other adults—parents most likely. "... extensive training and experience," she was saying. "So I'm hoping she'll be able to teach our students what they need to go on."

"Go on to what?" asked one man, who was dressed in blue jeans and a leather jacket.

"Well, certainly our Veronique has become very interested in auditioning for the National Ballet School. They have very high standards—a little too high, perhaps. But I'm sure Veronique can meet the bar, if she works hard."

Madame Beaufort glanced at her watch. "Time for class, I'm afraid." She said her good-byes and ushered Jenny toward the studio. "Nice to see you back, Jenny."

"Madame Beaufort," said Jenny, just before they reached the door, "I have to show you a note."

Jenny took a piece of paper from between the pages of her notebook and handed it to Madame Beaufort. It was the first time in her life she had ever forged anything. She held her breath anxiously as Madame Beaufort studied the note, which read,

Dear Madame Beaufort,

Please forgive Jenny for not participating in dance class on Saturday. We have taken her to the doctor, and he says she has vertigo caused by a viral infection. It should clear up in a few weeks. In the meantime, she's not supposed to do any dancing. Instead, could she please just sit and watch the dance classes and take notes so she doesn't fall too far behind?

Marilyn Spark

Jenny had looked up the causes of vertigo on the Internet in order to make the note more convincing.

"Vertigo?" said Madame Beaufort, frowning. She looked Jenny in the eye. "That's not contagious, is it?"

"Um, I don't think so," said Jenny. She hadn't anticipated that question.

"Well, I'm not sure how much good it would do you to just watch. Dancing is something your body must learn by doing. I wouldn't want your mother to feel she's wasting her money." She hesitated. "You could always wait and start dance next term, when you're fully recovered."

"Please," said Jenny, "I don't want to miss anything."

"Is your mother here?"

"No. She's at work." This statement was true at least.

"Does she know we usually don't give refunds after the second class?"

"Oh, yes, she knows. She doesn't mind." Then Jenny added, "She thinks it's really important that I take this class."

Madame Beaufort seemed to make up her mind reluctantly. "Well, I suppose you can observe the class today, and we'll see about after that. But you must sit quietly and not distract the other girls."

"Don't worry. I won't." Jenny exhaled in relief. She had bought herself some time.

Chapter 5

The New Teacher

In the studio, the students were sitting in a semicircle around a woman who was perched on a high wooden stool. Jenny realized she must be Katrina Miles. She looked a lot younger than Madame Beaufort and a lot thinner. Her dark brown hair was braided into two loops that hung from the back of her head. And unlike Madame Beaufort, she was dressed much like the students, in a navy leotard with a rehearsal skirt tied around her hips.

"Miss Miles," said Madame Beaufort, "this is Jenny Spark. She'll just be observing the class today."

Miss Miles gave Jenny a warm smile. "Hello, Jenny. Would you like to join us?"

Jenny hesitated and then glanced over to the piano.

"Or you can have a seat somewhere else if you like," said Miss Miles. Jenny sat down beside the piano.

After Madame Beaufort left the studio, Miss Miles had each of the students introduce themselves. Then she addressed the class. "First of all, you can call me Kat rather than Miss Miles if you prefer. I'll answer to either.

"Second, part of the purpose of this class is to extend the work you're doing in your regular Thursday and Saturday classes. So we're going to spend the first half of each class doing traditional ballet training, preparing you for the next level of exams, and then move on to something a little more interesting. Any questions?"

Lian's hand shot up immediately. "What do you mean by 'more interesting'?"

Kat, as Jenny decided to think of her, said, "Well, I understand in previous years, for your year-end recital, you've been focusing on scenes from classical ballet repertoire. Is that right?"

"Sort of," Lian replied.

"Well, I'm hoping this year we can create something original in class, something that might interest a wider audience."

"You mean the recital would be open to the public?"

"Yes, I mean exactly that."

Trish raised her hand. "But I thought the recitals were just for families to come to?"

"Well, yes, you can do a ballet recital that's just for family, if you just want to show your parents and grandparents how much you've learned over the course of a year. But ballet isn't just something we do for ourselves. Ballet is something we do to bring to the world a message or a story we feel passionate about. It's something to share with the whole community. One of the things I hope we'll do in this class is find the message you all want to share. Because if we do that, then this won't just be a ballet school. It will be a ballet company."

The next question was Ara's. "Will there be bigger parts for everybody?"

"Why do you ask?"

"Because last year there was only really one big part."

"Well, that's something that will depend on all of you. I have to see what everyone can do and what everyone wants to do. And we will have to see what we can create before we worry too much about casting."

From what Jenny could see, most of the class found Kat's ideas for the ballet exciting. The only two who didn't were Robyn, who seemed bored by the discussion, and Veronique, who looked rather put out.

As for Jenny, she liked this teacher. She could hardly wait to see what the class would create.

Kat continued. "Right now, however, let's begin with traditional ballet."

Kat put a CD of classical music on the stereo and led the class through a set of exercises similar to those in the previous class. Jenny took out her pen and wrote down the exercises in her notebook as best she could. She had to guess at the spelling. *Pliés, relevés, port de bras, battement*—there were so many new words to remember. At one point, she slid over to the sound system and stole a peek at the CD case. She wrote down the name of the music as well.

Kat spent a lot of time checking each student in turn, making sure everyone had the right posture and used the correct muscles. Every few minutes, however, she would slide back onto her stool, wincing slightly as she did so. Jenny thought Kat seemed more knowledgeable than Madame Beaufort. She worked the class a lot harder too.

Finally, Kat announced that it was time to try something new. "I assume you've all done some improvisation before, yes?"

Everyone looked at her blankly. "What's improvisation?" asked Kristen.

Kat looked surprised. "You must have done exercises in class sometimes when you made up your own steps to music?"

Again, blank stares.

"Well, perhaps this will be a new experience," Kat concluded. "Here's what I would like you to do. Find a spot on the floor with some space around you."

Everyone took their positions. Kat went over to the stereo.

"Now, when I start the music, I want you all to just close your eyes and listen closely for a moment. Once you've got a feel for the music, I'll ask you to start moving."

When the music began, Jenny closed her eyes too. It was an instrumental piece she had never heard before. It reminded her of a snake charmer.

Softly, Kat spoke over the music, "Now, with your eyes closed, just start to move your arms. Just your arms."

Jenny was tempted for a second to move her arms, but instead she opened her eyes and looked around. Everyone was responding to the music differently. Some were hesitant, as though worried about doing it right. Others moved mechanically, without any real connection to the music.

"Now open your eyes," said Kat, "and begin to move however you like."

With their eyes open, most people's movements became tentative. Veronique, although she moved gracefully, seemed to be repeating some of the steps the class had been practising earlier. *They look a bit like I felt during the first class,* Jenny thought. She sat up a little higher.

And then Jenny noticed Ara. Alone among the class, Ara did

not seem the least bit tentative or cautious. She looked like she was having fun.

In fact, the longer the music went on, the more confident Ara became. She began to skip, glide, even jump across the floor. While Veronique looked as though she had rehearsed her routine ahead of time, Ara's dancing was completely unpredictable and her pace altered with every change in the music.

Wow, thought Jenny. *I wish I could dance like that, like I didn't care what anyone thought.* Ara was like a bird set free from its cage, like a dolphin playing in the waves. At least, she did until one awkward moment when she fell over with a loud bang on the floor. But then she quickly rose to her feet and continued to dance.

When the music ended, Jenny felt disappointed. "Wha-hoo!" Ara exclaimed. "Can we do that again?"

Kat smiled. "Good work everyone. Not bad for your first time. With practice, you'll find it becomes easier." She glanced at her watch. "I'm afraid that's all the time we have for today. So let's end with *reverence*." Kat demonstrated an elaborate curtsey—*plieing* with her left foot, right foot behind, arms down and wide apart. The girls copied her.

"And for our gentleman," Kat continued, "a bow." Again, she demonstrated the proper movement. The only boy in the class, whose name was Lawrence, returned the bow.

"I'll see you all next week," Kat concluded. The class applauded.

As Ara started to leave, Kat stopped her. "You've got good instincts for improvisation. Very expressive. But I would like you to pay a little more attention to how you execute each movement so you don't overextend yourself."

"Thanks." Ara beamed. "I can hardly wait to try it again." She dashed out the door.

Before leaving, Jenny paused to go over her notes, so she was able to hear Veronique speak to Kat after the other students had gone.

"How did I do?" Veronique asked.

"Your technique is very good," Kat answered. "You just need to let yourself loosen up a bit. Don't worry. It will come with practice."

Veronique looked slightly disappointed, but she continued. "Miss Miles?"

"Yes," said Kat.

"I was wondering if I could ask a favour. My mom bought these for me." Veronique opened her dance bag and pulled out a pair of ballet shoes. They were not slippers, but pointe shoes—the kind ballerinas use to dance on their toes. Jenny had seen some on display in the dance supply store.

Kat studied the shoes carefully. "That's a good brand. But you probably should have waited until next term before being fitted. We probably won't do any pointe work until then."

"Well, see, my mom thought I could ask you if you could give me some exercises I could practise at home. You know, to get a head start. I'm auditioning for the National Ballet Summer Programme, and I really want to get in."

Kat gave Veronique a serious look. "No, I'm sorry. You mustn't try to do pointe work on your own. I need time to evaluate your strength and skill level. And you need to learn the correct technique. Otherwise, you could do serious damage to your feet and ankles, and then you wouldn't be able to dance at all—let alone pass an audition. I'll help you when you're ready. But not until then."

Veronique looked frustrated. "But my mother said ..."

"I'll talk to your mother," Kat assured her. "I'll make sure she understands. Don't be disappointed. It's better in the long run. You have to learn to float before you swim."

Veronique seemed to accept defeat. "Okay," she said and stuffed the shoes back into her bag.

"Okay," said Kat. "See you next week."

Jenny found her father waiting in the car outside the ballet school. She jumped in.

"How did today go?" her father asked.

"Even better than Saturday," Jenny replied. She could hardly believe her plan was working so perfectly.

Chapter 6

The Accident

Jenny felt that the next few classes went extremely well. Madame Beaufort and Kat sometimes asked her how she was feeling, and she was careful to always say, "A little dizzy, but okay."

Gradually, Jenny got used to being around the other students and managed to say hi to them sometimes, as long as they said hi first. Ara was very friendly. But then, she was friendly to everyone, even those who weren't quite as friendly in return.

Even though Jenny didn't dance in class, she continued to change into her dance outfit each time. Dressing like the other girls made her feel as though she was a part of the class. Besides, Jenny thought her mother might suspect something if the leotard and tights remained clean and fresh looking class after class. So each night, Jenny would put them on and practise the exercises from the previous class in her room (at least the ones she could do easily; Kat's words of warning to Veronique still echoed in her head). It wasn't long before Jenny began noticing muscles in her legs she didn't know she had before.

One Sunday afternoon, Jenny saw her father putting a cardboard box down in the front hall.

"What's in the box?" Jenny asked.

"Oh, just some old junk from my office," he answered. "I need more space. So I think I'll donate it."

Jenny looked inside and saw an old camcorder. "Hey," she said. "Does this still work?"

"Oh, yes, it records all right, in DVD format. But just thirty minutes a disc. And you can't re-record." He added, "This is what we used to make videos of you as a baby."

Jenny had an idea. "Can I have it?"

"Sure, if you want. Got a film project in mind?"

"Thinking of one."

Jenny's father helped her find a blank DVD and made sure the battery pack in the camcorder was working. Then Jenny stuck the camcorder in her dance bag.

At dance class the next day, Jenny took her dance bag, along with the camcorder, into the studio. Her idea was to secretly video parts of the class so she could review them at home and make sure she was doing the exercises correctly. Every now and then, when no one was looking, she would sneak her hand into her bag, press the record button, and lift the camcorder just high enough for the lens to capture what everyone was doing.

As usual for a Monday, Kat was teaching, and the second half of the class was devoted to improvisation. Today, however, there was no music. Instead, Kat had brought in an electronic metronome, which she placed on the piano next to her stool.

"Here's what I would like everyone to do," Kat explained. "I will start the metronome, beating out a rhythm. Every now and then, I will change the speed of the rhythm from fast to slow to everything in between. You can move any way you like as long as you follow these two rules. Number one, you must move in time with the metronome. Number two, you can't stop moving until I say so."

Kat started the metronome off at a slow, steady beat. It took the class a minute or so to get into the exercise. But soon everyone was moving in sync with the beat.

"Now, whatever you do," Kat called out, "don't stop. Keep moving to the rhythm."

From her usual spot by the piano, Jenny watched everyone cope with the rules of the exercise. Because they had to keep moving, most students chose to walk or run in time with the beat. It was an easy choice, but it became boring quickly. So Kat began telling students to explore other ways of moving and use other parts of their bodies.

Soon students were nodding their heads, waving their hands, rolling their shoulders, or doing odd combinations of movements and steps. They began to have fun seeing how many different ways they could move without breaking the rhythm.

As usual, Ara was the one to watch. She not only stayed in motion, but it was never the same motion. She constantly changed directions and changed which body parts were involved in the movement. One moment she'd be sliding on the floor, and the next she'd be leaping through the air. Sometimes she'd deliberately shadow other students or dance in front of them so they would have to react to her, to dance with her. It was as though she wanted to see how far she could push the rules.

Only Veronique, as usual, seemed to be having trouble letting herself go. Every movement she made was graceful and balanced.

She pirouetted when the tempo was fast and executed perfect *adagios*—slow, graceful movements—when the tempo crawled. But she never seemed to be making it up as she went along. *She's not really improvising*, Jenny thought. *It's more like she's performing.* But it was a dazzling performance.

How the accident actually happened was unclear at first. The metronome was beating out a fairly fast rhythm at the time, which certainly didn't help. Ara was dancing by herself for the moment in one corner of the studio. And she was dancing brilliantly, Jenny thought. From the opposite corner, Veronique began to dance a series of pirouettes, crossing the floor on a diagonal toward Ara's corner. Jenny had aimed the camcorder to take in both of them, totally captivated by what each was doing. Just then Lian sailed past the piano doing a series of big, expressive leaps. Jenny turned her head to follow Lian.

A second later, Jenny heard a loud whack, followed by a thud and a sharp cry of pain. She turned her head and saw Veronique sitting on the floor, her hand pressed over her left eye, and Ara kneeling beside her.

Kat shut off the metronome immediately, slid off her stool, and ran to see what had happened. So did everyone else. Ara was apologizing profusely over and over as she offered to help Veronique stand up. Apparently, she and Veronique had collided. Veronique swore loudly at Ara, using some choice words Jenny didn't know but that sounded French. Veronique grabbed Kat's arm with her free hand and pulled herself to her feet. Kat winced and asked Ara to get an ice pack from the small refrigerator in the office and to fetch Madame Beaufort.

When Ara returned with the ice pack and Madame, Veronique

was still inconsolable. She held the ice pack against her sore eye while her mother put an arm around her and took her to the office to lie down.

Later, in the girls' change room, Robyn explained why her sister was so upset. "She has an audition coming up. Well, it's a workshop by the National Ballet School. But if she does well, they'll let her into their summer programme. She'll be really ticked if she has to show up with a black eye."

Lian, who was just beginning to don her usual layers of street clothes, immediately turned to Ara. "Why didn't you watch what you were doing? Veronique must be devastated."

Ara, who had just finished pulling a sweater and jeans over her leotard, looked a little devastated too. "I didn't know she was anywhere near me," she explained. "I had my back to her. I was just improvising. She must have seen me. Why did she come so close?"

"How was Veronique supposed to know you were going to fling your arm out?" said Kristen. "Maybe if you danced a little slower …"

"Of course she didn't know what I was going to do," Ara protested. "I didn't know what I going to do until I did it. That's what improvisation is, right? I was just following the rhythm. It was a fast beat."

No one else said anything. But judging by the looks on everyone's faces, Jenny didn't think Ara had anyone's sympathy.

Ara threw her coat on over her dance gear and bolted out the door before another word was spoken.

For the first time in the change room, Jenny got up the courage to speak. "It was an accident, wasn't it?"

Lian turned to her, a little surprised to hear Jenny's voice. "I didn't actually see what happened. Did anyone else?"

No one spoke.

"Thing is," Lian explained, "it's not the first accident Ara's had. She's got a bit of a talent for them."

"She just gets a little carried away sometimes," Trish explained. "And she forgets to pay attention to things. But I don't think she means any harm."

"Remember what happened at the dress rehearsal for last year's recital?" Kristen said, smiling to the room at large. Then she turned to Jenny. "We all had to dance offstage at one point. But the wing was crowded, so the people at the end of the line had to slow down until the space cleared and there was room. Ara was the last one off, but she got so carried away with her performance that she tried to exit at full speed."

Trish interrupted, laughing. "And then she tripped over Lian, ran smack into the wall, and hit the fire alarm!"

Lian started laughing too. "Remember the look on Madame Beaufort's face! It's just a good thing it wasn't the actual performance." Then she looked at Jenny again. "Word of advice. If you ever have to be in a recital with her, try to be on the opposite side of the stage."

It wasn't until later that evening, when she was getting ready to do her nightly exercises, that Jenny remembered the DVD. She took the camcorder out of her dance bag. Then she removed the disc and popped it into her DVD player. Fast-forwarding to the end, she discovered that the camcorder had captured the accident perfectly.

Jenny watched as Veronique approached Ara, spinning around on what was likely her last pirouette before reaching the corner. Suddenly, Ara made a sidestep in Veronique's direction, flinging her arms out at the same time in a rather fast *port de bras.* That was when the back of Ara's right hand connected with Veronique's eye.

Jenny felt sorry for both girls. But as she watched the recording for a second time, she realized something. Ara had clearly been focused on her dancing and having a lot of fun. She certainly was not worrying about who was near her. But that was because, as far as she knew, no one was near her. There were no mirrors in that corner, and Ara definitely had her back to Veronique, just as she had said. There was no way she could have seen Veronique coming.

On the other hand, Veronique may have been pirouetting, but she was using a ballet technique called spotting to prevent herself from getting dizzy. During each twirl, she kept her eyes focused on a spot directly ahead of her—only whipping her head around at the last second to focus on the same spot again. What's more, the spot she was focusing on was very much in Ara's direction. Veronique must have seen she was getting close to Ara. And she must have known Ara's movements were likely to be unpredictable. The only explanation, Jenny thought, was that it wasn't Ara but Veronique who wasn't paying attention.

Jenny felt glad to have discovered the truth. Somehow, she wanted Ara to be free of blame, partly because Ara was friendlier toward her than Veronique was and partly because she just loved watching Ara dance. It seemed strange to her that everyone admired Veronique's dancing but not Ara's.

Jenny remembered the look on Ara's face when no one believed her. If she felt guilty, would she be afraid to improvise next time, afraid to cause another accident? Would she worry so much about keeping out of everyone's way that she wouldn't dance in that wildly fun and inventive way anymore?

Chapter 7

A New Friend

As it turned out, before Jenny had a chance to tell Ara about the video, a new problem arose. On Wednesday morning, as Jenny was packing her ballet bag by the front door—her schoolbag, already packed, sat on the tiled floor beside it—her mother called from the kitchen. "Jenny, could you come here for a minute? There's something I'd like to ask you."

In the kitchen, Jenny found her mother wearing her usual Wednesday suit, sitting at the table with her morning paper. Her father was busy packing his lunch into a leather satchel. He had classes at the Faculty of Education that day.

"What is it?" Jenny asked.

"I was just wondering how you're getting along at your dance lessons," her mother explained.

"Fine," said Jenny. "I mean, good."

"Made any new friends?"

Instantly, Jenny's mind jumped to a higher state of alert. This was a topic she had been hoping to avoid. There was only one way to answer, and that was with a lie. And despite her actions over the past few weeks, Jenny hated lying to her parents. She would have preferred to avoid the issue. But if she told her mother that after three weeks of classes she hadn't made a single friend, her mother might change her mind about letting her take dance.

"Oh, sure," she said, trying to sound casual.

Jenny's father straightened and looked over at Jenny. He must have been curious too.

"Anyone we could meet sometime?" asked her mother.

So this was what her mother had in mind. Jenny frantically searched her brain for a way to deal with this request. There was no logical reason why she couldn't introduce her mother to a friend, apart from the truth that she hadn't made any friends. All she could do was tell another little lie in hopes of delaying her inevitable doom.

"Sure, I suppose so," Jenny replied.

"What's her name?" her mother asked.

A new option—changing the subject—now sprang to Jenny's mind. She wished she had thought of it a few seconds sooner.

"Dad!" Jenny shouted, "It's twenty minutes past eight! You said you'd drive me to school."

Her father glanced at the clock. "Oops, you're right. We'd better go." He slung his satchel over his shoulder and followed Jenny quickly to the front door. Jenny grabbed her schoolbag, and they both left.

After school, Jenny's mother picked her up to take her to dance class. She had brought the dance bag Jenny had left in the front hall.

As she drove, Jenny's mother raised the same subject again. "I was hoping you could introduce me to your friend today."

"Um, I'm not sure she's going to be there today," said Jenny.

"Well, I'll be in the waiting room when the class ends just in case. But if not today, then next time."

Jenny entered the dance school, accompanied by both her mother and a new feeling of dread. She had won a slight reprieve at best. Today's class might be her last—unless, of course, she could make a new friend in the next hour or so. As her mother sat down on one of the couches in the waiting room, Jenny went to get changed, feeling not very hopeful.

Luckily, something happened that took Jenny's mind temporarily off her worry.

It started in the change room. Veronique was absent that day, and Robyn explained that she was home nursing her injured eye. "It's not really that bad. If she didn't insist on keeping this huge bandage over it, you would hardly notice it at all."

"Is she still going to her audition?" Lian asked.

"Oh, yeah. Her plan now is to put makeup over the bruise. I suggested a goalie mask, but she didn't go for it."

At that moment, there was a soft thudding on the door. Lian opened it and found Ara standing there with her arms encased in what looked like foam rubber batons.

"What are those?" Lian asked in amazement.

"What do you think?" Ara asked. "I found some old foam bats in our basement. I took the stick part out, shoved my hands in instead, and voila—now if someone bangs into my hand, they won't get hurt!"

Ara looked so ridiculous that everyone had to smile, even though the idea that she expected to have other accidents seemed in poor taste.

Glen C. Strathy

"You'd better not hit anyone else," Trish commented.

"I don't plan to," said Ara. "But what can I do about Veronique? I can't undo what happened. I thought about finding her a helmet, but she'd never fit her bun under it."

"She's not here anyway," said Lian. Then after a pause she added, "But maybe she'd like a nice pair of sunglasses."

Madame Beaufort was teaching the class today, so there was no improvisation. But Ara's playfulness was so irrepressible that there may as well have been. Madame Beaufort made her take the foam batons off her hands, to no one's great surprise. But Ara continued to do everything she could to make her fellow students laugh. During stretching exercises, she rolled around the floor, banging into the people beside her. At the barre, whenever Madame Beaufort wasn't looking, she did little bits of pantomime and made faces in the mirror so the others could see.

As Ara's antics were the most interesting part of the class that day, Jenny watched her constantly. All the while, she kept thinking about how she would have reacted had she accidentally hurt someone. If anything, Jenny would have felt too ashamed to show her face, let alone seek out extra attention. But Ara seemed determined to make everyone forgive her through sheer persistent charm.

The last straw broke when the class ended. Ara reached the change room ahead of everyone else and bonked each person on the head with her foam batons as they came through the door.

"Hey, Ara," said Kristen once everyone was in. "Can I see those bats for a moment?"

"Sure," said Ara, and she handed them over.

Kristen handed one bat to Robyn and said, "Ready?"

"Ready," said Robyn. And the two girls proceeded to get their revenge by bonking Ara several times each. Ara squealed with laughter as she raised her arms over her head to defend herself.

"Ara, you're just too out of control!" yelled Kristen, throwing down her bat. "You should be more like Jenny. Then we could have a serious class!"

"Yeah," Lian chimed in, "and maybe Jenny should be more like Ara. Then maybe she'd actually enjoy the class."

Jenny stopped pulling bunpins out of her hair. She looked at Lian and in a small voice said, "I do enjoy the class."

"Yeah, well, you'd never know it." Lian turned to Kristen. "You know, I think you're right. Maybe if Jenny and Ara could change places for a week, things would even out around here. Ara would have to chill out a little, and Jenny would have to dance."

Jenny looked over at Ara, whose giggling was finally subsiding. Their eyes made contact for a second, and in that moment they felt a flash of understanding. Lian, they realized, might have a point.

After changing and running a comb through her hair, Jenny slung her dance bag over her shoulder and got up to leave. Then she remembered. Her mother would be waiting just down the hall. Jenny turned and sat down again. In an instant, she decided on a plan. She would wait in the change room until all the other girls had left. Then when she went out, she could say her friend had already gone.

"Hey, what's up?" Ara had come over and was looking down at her. "You went pale all of the sudden. Are you feeling all right? Is it the vertigo?"

Jenny tried to smile but had a feeling it didn't come out right. Looking at Ara's carefree face, framed by her black pigtails, Jenny realized there was no way Ara would understand her predicament. If Ara was in her shoes, she would think of something funny and spontaneous that would get her off the hook. Come to think of it, Ara probably wouldn't care whether she was on the hook or not. That girl was a wild fish—totally hook-free.

Jenny shook her head. "I can't explain."

Ara sat down. "Try me."

Jenny took a deep breath and decided to risk it. "My mother's waiting for me in the waiting room."

"Good spot for it," said Ara.

"She wants me to introduce her to someone I've made friends with in dance class. If I don't, she'll make me quit coming."

"No problem," said Ara without a moment's hesitation. "I like meeting people's parents."

Jenny blinked. Then she frowned. Then she asked, "Really?"

Ara took Jenny by the arm and half pulled her down the hall. Jenny could not believe this was happening. She could see no reason why Ara would be willing to call her a friend when they hardly knew each other or to do her such a huge favour.

Jenny's mother was standing by the notice board, looking at a pamphlet. Ara's mother was sitting on a chair, flipping through a magazine.

"Is that your mom?" Ara whispered to Jenny.

"Yes," Jenny whispered back.

Ara bounded forward. "Are you Mrs. Spark?"

Jenny's mother smiled. "Yes."

"I'm Ara Reyes, Jenny's friend. I was wondering if I could ask Jenny to come to my house for dinner today?" Turning to her mother, Ara added, "Is that okay, Mom?"

Both mothers looked at each other. "Sure," said Mrs. Reyes. She stood up and offered Jenny's mother her hand. "I'm Eman Reyes."

Jenny's mother shook Eman's hand. "I'm Marilyn Spark. It's so nice to meet you."

"Oh, everyone says that. But your daughter is certainly welcome to come to dinner."

Before Jenny knew what was happening, her mother had exchanged addresses and phone numbers with Ara's mother, and Ara was pulling her out the front door towards the Reyeses' car.

Chapter 8

Opposites

Jenny sat in the back seat with Ara, feeling both grateful and nervous at the same time.

"Thanks for inviting me," Jenny said.

"No problem," Ara replied. "This'll be fun."

"I actually wanted to tell you something."

"What?"

"That accident you had with Veronique, I know it wasn't your fault."

"No kidding!" Ara exploded. "I didn't mean to hit her. I never saw her coming. She just ran into me without looking! She acts like she owns the studio and like everyone should just know to keep out of her way. Honestly! And she doesn't even improvise anyway. All she does is repeat the same steps we do all the time. It's so weird. She could be an okay person, except her mother has her convinced she's, like, a prima ballerina, so she has to keep showing off all the time to maintain her status."

"You could learn a few things from Veronique," said Mrs. Reyes from the front seat.

"Mother!" Ara protested, leaning forward. "She dances like a machine!"

"A beautiful machine."

"A machine that has no *feeling*!"

Jenny had a feeling this conversation was going to turn into a shouting match in a few seconds. "Veronique can do the steps more perfectly than anyone, but I think you're the most interesting dancer in the class. I love to watch you."

Ara turned back to Jenny. "Really?"

"That's very nice of you to say," said Mrs. Reyes, looking at Jenny through the rearview mirror.

"It's true," Jenny continued.

"You know, Mom," said Ara, "Jenny is the only girl in the class who never dances."

Uh-oh, Jenny thought. *Please don't spill my secret.*

"Really?" asked Mrs. Reyes. "Why not?"

"Um," Jenny answered, "I've been a little sick lately. So I've just been learning what I can by watching—until I'm feeling better."

"Well, I hope you feel better soon," said Mrs. Reyes. "Time marches on. Here we are."

Mrs. Reyes turned the car into a driveway and brought it to a stop.

"Wow," said Jenny, realizing this was Ara's house, "you don't live too far from me. I recognize the video store on the corner."

"That's the one my parents own," Ara explained. "Come on in."

Jenny followed Ara into the house. As they were taking off their shoes, a girl who looked about sixteen came running down the stairs.

"Ara, you have to skip dance class next Thursday," the girl said. She was barefooted, with fuchsia-painted toenails, and wearing low-rise jeans beneath a very tight T-shirt. Enormous gold earrings were almost hidden under her wavy, dark hair.

"I can't," was Ara's flat reply.

"You have to. Dad wants you to help him do inventory."

"Why can't you?"

"Because I have to work on a project with Ashley for school that day."

Ara threw her hands into the air. "Aaaaarrrrr! Mother, she's doing it again."

Mrs. Reyes, who had just come through the front door in time to hear the end of this conversation said, "Nadda, you know your sister can't miss ballet."

"Why not? It's not like she's the star or anything." To Ara, Nadda added, "Practising for the chorus again?"

"It's *corps de ballet*. Choruses are for singers," said Ara. "And I can't miss class if I want to get good."

"Maybe you're as good as you'll ever get."

"You're just being selfish because you hate helping at the store!" Ara was shouting now.

"Yeah, so do you!" Nadda shouted back.

"Those are cool earrings!" Jenny suddenly said. *Anything to change the subject*, she thought.

Nadda burst into a smile and looked at Jenny for the first time. "Aren't they? I found them at this great store on Princess Street." Turning back to Ara, she added, "Who's your friend?"

"This is Jenny," said Ara. "Jenny, this is my sister, Nadda. Come on, let's go see if dinner's ready."

Dinner took place without any further arguments. Jenny discovered at the table that Ara had two brothers as well, Ben and Jerad, both younger than her. She also discovered that as prone to arguing as the Reyeses were, they were equally prone to laughter, and there were quite a few jokes told during the meal.

When dessert was finished, Ara invited Jenny to see her room. As soon as they reached the upstairs, Jenny knew which door was Ara's. It had a huge piece of Bristol board taped on the outside, with the words, "Not today! I have ballet!" written on it in thick marker. Inside, Ara's room was messy and chaotic, just as Jenny had expected. But Ara cleared a space on the bed for the two of them to sit.

"I'm glad you said it wasn't my fault about Veronique's eye," said Ara.

"Actually, I have it on video," said Jenny. "She wasn't looking at all."

"Really? Well, that could be handy, since I don't think anyone else believes it," Ara said, a note of sadness in her voice. "Do you really like the way I dance? Or were you just being nice?"

"I do," said Jenny.

Ara paused for a moment. "Thing is, this could be my last year in ballet."

Jenny felt disappointed by this bit of news. "Why?"

"My dad doesn't think he should keep spending money on dance lessons. He keeps wanting me to help out more at the store. He says it would be different if I was dancing a solo or something, but there's not much chance of that with Veronique around. She always gets the principal roles."

"Always?"

Ara shrugged. "For as long as the school's been around, and that's four years so far."

"Wow. So you've been in the school since it started?"

"Yep. Me and Veronique and Lian. We started the same year." Ara hesitated, as though for once she was not sure she should say what was on her mind. "Lian's weird. You know she takes singing and drama lessons as well as ballet?"

"Cool," said Jenny. She wondered how Lian had the time.

"She says you never know when a great opportunity will come along, so she wants to be prepared. She thinks some talent agent might come to Kingston one day, spot her, and make her a star."

"I guess there's a chance," said Jenny.

"Thing is, she got me thinking about other unlikely events." Ara hesitated again. "See, there's this scholarship the school gives each year to, like, the most improved student out of all the classes. Of course, Veronique always gets that too."

Jenny was outraged. "That's not fair! Veronique's mom is a teacher. She must get lessons for free anyway!"

"I know. She says she's saving the money to go to a better dance school. Thing is, I just wish everything didn't have to be about who's the best. I wish we could do a ballet where everyone had decent roles and could do the steps they were best at. Then maybe everyone could get a scholarship because everyone would stand out. I'm actually hoping Veronique gets into National because then someone else might have a chance."

"You could do it," Jenny said.

"Do what?"

"You could be a principal. You've got great instincts. Kat said so."

Ara shrugged. "Well, that would show my dad. But I don't think I could do what Veronique does. Now, if we could *improvise* in the recital, that would be cool."

Ara paused, and then it was her turn to have an idea. "Hey, you could do it!"

"Do what?"

"You could be the most improved student! As soon as you're feeling better. Because you'd be going from not dancing to dancing, and that would be a bigger improvement than anyone!"

Jenny dropped her gaze to the floor and began twisting her hair. "I don't think I could do that."

"Why not? You'll be feeling better soon, won't you?"

Jenny hesitated. "If I tell you something, can you promise to keep it a secret?"

"Sure," said Ara.

"I mean really promise?"

"Sure."

"The truth is, I'm not really sick. I mean, I sort of am, but it's not like a real sickness. The truth is, I'm afraid to dance."

"Afraid to dance?" Ara sounded astonished, as though she couldn't imagine such a thing. "But dancing is so much fun."

"You and everyone else have been dancing for years. I just don't think I could do it like you. I don't want anyone to see me try."

Ara took a few seconds to digest this idea. "Wow," she said. "So, did your parents, like, make you sign up?"

"Oh, no. I wanted it. I love ballet—more than anything. I just can't do it in front of people."

Again, Ara was silent for a moment. "You know what," she said at last, "Kristen was right. We should be more alike. If you were more like me, maybe then you could dance and not care. And if I were more like you, maybe I wouldn't fight with my family so much. Then again, in this house, you don't get much by keeping quiet."

"If you were a bit more like me, you wouldn't be such a wild fish. You might slow down and master a few of the steps Veronique is so good at. But," Jenny added quickly, "you wouldn't want to be like me. It's not much fun."

"I don't know." Ara seemed to be thinking. "Show me how."

"What?"

"Show me how to be like you. So I can see how it feels."

Jenny had never tried to explain how it was to be her before. "I don't know how."

Ara jumped off the bed and walked to the door. "Okay, pretend I'm you walking into the dance studio." She mimed walking in the door, head down, twisting a lock of hair around her forefinger. "What am I doing wrong?"

Jenny laughed and then began to study her. "Well, to start with, you're walking too fast. You're worried about who might be in the room already and whether they like you enough to want you to be there. You figure they probably don't, so you go slow and hope to sneak in without attracting too much attention so they won't notice you and start making fun of you."

Ara tried it again more slowly. "Okay, what else?"

"You need to hang your head a little lower to one side. Close your body in a bit more. Try to make yourself invisible."

Ara changed her body language to match Jenny's description.

"Now look for a spot to sit away from everyone else, where you can feel completely hidden but watch everything."

Ara plonked herself down in a corner. "Now what?"

"Now, when everyone dances, you let your heart dance with them."

Ara held still for a moment, trying to put her all her concentration on being Jenny. Then she jumped to her feet, took two quick steps, and landed on the bed. "No, you're right. I can't do it. If someone's dancing, I have to dance too."

"See what I mean?"

"Anyway, now it's your turn."

Jenny froze. "My turn?"

"Yeah, your turn to be me."

"I couldn't."

"Sure you can. I'll coach you."

Jenny slowly got to her feet and went to the door. Then she hesitated. "I'm not sure what to do."

"How do I come into a room?" Ara asked.

Jenny thought. "Well, you sort of explode in. Kind of like …" She started to mime flinging herself into the room. But halfway through, she suddenly thought about Ara looking at her and wondered what Ara thought and how stupid she must look. Immediately, she pulled her arms in and sat back down on the bed. "No. I can't be you either."

"Too bad," said Ara. "It sounded like a good idea for a minute. You wanna play a game or something?"

"Sure."

Ara led Jenny to the cupboard that housed the Reyes family's collection of board games. They chose one they both liked and took it to the basement rec room. Ara's brothers and sister decided to play too. By the time Jenny's mother arrived to take her home, Jenny was very sorry to go.

Chapter 9

Discovery

After Jenny's evening at the Reyeses', her mother stopped pestering her about making friends. And for the first time in a long time, Jenny felt she actually had one.

Miraculously, as the weeks passed, neither of the teachers at the Kingston Ballet School seemed to wonder why Jenny was taking so long to get over her case of vertigo. At least, they never asked Jenny's parents about her health.

Jenny continued to repeat each ballet class at home in the sanctuary of her room, using her notes, sketches, and now the occasional bit of video. That is, she did as much as she could. There was barely enough space in her room to do two pirouettes in a row, and her dresser handles made a poor substitute for a barre. Nonetheless, her body grew stronger and more flexible. She could stretch past her toes now and practise the positions with greater turnout. The muscles on her calves and in other places became firmer. These changes pleased her, and Jenny found she was enjoying the life of a secret ballerina.

It wasn't until one Friday in late October that her mother dropped another bombshell.

Jenny was lying on the living room floor after dinner, flipping channels on the TV, when her mother folded her newspaper, settled back on the couch, and said, "So, Jenny, I see your dance school is having an open house event tomorrow."

Jenny's mouth fell open, and she turned to her mother. "A what?" she asked.

"An open house. The day parents are invited to come and watch the classes. I've been looking forward to seeing you dance after all these weeks."

"Um, you don't really want to see me dance."

"Yes, I do. And your father wants to as well. Why? There's nothing wrong, is there?"

Jenny felt a rush of panic coursing through her brain. The room began to spin ever so slightly. "No," she managed to say. *Just the end of my days as a dance student*, she thought. *Just total utter humiliation.*

On Saturday morning, Jenny dragged herself downstairs, bleary-eyed from lack of sleep. She had lain awake the entire night, trying unsuccessfully to come up with a plan to stop her parents from discovering that she hadn't been dancing in class.

The only possible solution Jenny could see was to try, for the first time, to participate in the class—after explaining to Madame Beaufort and all the other students, while her mother was out of earshot, that she had made a miraculous recovery, and at the same time asking them not to say anything about her two-month-long illness in front of her parents. As plans went, this one seemed to have a few holes.

Because even if she succeeded in keeping her lies a secret, and even though she now knew many of the exercises by heart, she still didn't think she could actually perform them in front of people—let alone a crowd of parents she didn't know very well.

Sitting in the back seat of the car, Jenny felt a flood of disappointment as her father turned the ignition key and the engine roared to life. Mechanical failure had been her last hope.

During the drive over, Jenny kept running over in her mind the sequence of a typical class. Barre work, stretches, adagios, pirouettes, allegros. Would Madame Beaufort teach anything new in an open house class? Probably not. But could Jenny actually bring herself to do the steps she knew? Definitely not.

When they finally arrived at the school, the crowd in the waiting room was swollen to twice the usual number of parents and siblings—all there for the open house, no doubt.

Kat was standing near the door, chatting with some of the adults. Jenny's mother went up to her immediately and told her how much she was looking forward to seeing the class.

Jenny tensed, fearing the truth would come out then and there. But instead, Kat smiled and said, "Yes, well normally I wouldn't be teaching at all today, but the girls really wanted the chance to let their parents see some of the more improvisational work we've been doing in the Monday classes. I'm trying to give the students a chance to develop their artistry as well as technical proficiency. If all goes well, I'd like the class to develop an original performance piece for the spring recital …"

This was even worse than Jenny had imagined. If she was 99 percent certain she couldn't dance ballet in front of this crowd, she was 200 percent certain she couldn't improvise in front of them.

And what would her mother say afterward? Not only would she take away the dance lessons, she would know that Jenny had been lying to her for months. She would know that Jenny was inconsiderate, dishonest, and talentless as well.

Jenny had to get out of the congested room. She said good-bye to her parents and headed down the hall. Maybe she could just stay in the girls' change room until ... well, actually, forever sounded good.

But when she got to the change room, Lian and Kristen were there, and so was Lian's mother, Mrs. Peng, who was just saying good-bye. So much for that plan. If mothers were allowed in, the change room would not be a safe place to hide during class.

Out of habit, Jenny changed into her dance outfit. She waited until everyone, parents and students, had left for the studio. Then she quietly stepped into the hall and walked to the studio door, which had been left open. Her curiosity, as usual, made her want to see what the class was doing. Fortunately, her parents were nowhere near the door, and the spectators nearest her had their back to her.

Unfortunately, Jenny couldn't see very much. But she could hear Madame Beaufort saying something to the parents about the spring recital. What would her parents be thinking now, looking at the class and seeing Jenny absent? Would they be wondering where she was, if anything had happened to her? Would they come looking for her?

Jenny backed away from the door. She was starting to feel light-headed again. She needed somewhere to hide, perhaps some fresh air. There was the door to the girls' change room (not a great option), the door to the waiting room (that didn't feel good either), and a door marked "Fire Exit." She decided to take the plunge.

In hindsight, Jenny should have remembered that fire doors are often connected to alarm systems. However, once she found herself standing on the fire escape, with a loud clanging coming from over her right shoulder, it was too late to change her mind. She shoved the door closed behind her. Glancing out over the railing, she could see the shore of Lake Ontario. It looked calm and cool, but Jenny's main concern was to get away before the alarm brought other people onto the fire escape. Fortunately, it was an easy journey down the wobbly metal steps to the ground. The wear and tear on her ballet slippers as she ran along the gravelled alleyway couldn't be helped. Anyway, the soles had looked practically new for far too long.

All she could think about was making sure no one knew she had set off the alarm. She made it around the corner of the building and over to the steps that led to the front door. Perhaps she could convince her parents she had been on her way to class when she heard the alarm and went outside.

She couldn't hear the clanging anymore. And there didn't seem to be anyone coming out. So Jenny sat down on the steps to wait.

Now that she was still, Jenny felt the cool October air penetrate her thin leotard. She hugged her legs against her chest. The step she sat on felt as cold as ice. After some time, she began to feel a little calmer, but a numbness was spreading through her toes, fingers, and seat, and her body began to shiver. Finally, she couldn't take it anymore. She walked up the stairs, teeth chattering, and went inside.

The hall was full of parents and students. Was the class already over? Nobody looked panicked, and they weren't all heading for the door. The alarm wasn't ringing. Maybe it shut off when she closed the door? That was lucky. It explained why no fire trucks had come sirening up to the building while Jenny had sat out front. The class must have just continued as planned.

The warmth of the building felt wonderful, and Jenny's body began to relax a little. Timidly, she walked along the hallway in the direction of the dance school, rubbing her hands and arms and trying to blend into the crowd. She would have to face her parents now. There was no other choice.

Zigzagging past people, Jenny saw her father first. He was standing with his back to her. She walked up to him and almost tapped him on the shoulder before she realized he was deep in conversation with Madame Beaufort, who had a very displeased look on her face. Jenny turned her back on both of them, suddenly afraid they were talking about her. She listened for a moment, just to make sure.

"I thought the improvisation was really interesting," her father was saying.

"Yes, well, I think they've done quite enough of that for the time being," Madame Beaufort replied. "What the girls really need at their age is to develop strength, control, and an understanding of the classical repertoire. That's where the real beauty of ballet is. I know that's what has helped Veronique the most. Too much of what we saw today can actually shortchange a dancer's development. Besides which, the risk of injury is so much greater. So I think I'll have to insist that Katrina take a more traditional approach when it comes to the spring recital ..."

Jenny wasn't used to teachers criticizing other teachers this way, especially in front of students and parents. She had a feeling that Madame Beaufort wanted to vent her annoyance so much she didn't care who was listening.

There was no telling how long Madame would go on, and Jenny was in no hurry to speak to her father. So she decided to make her way to the girls' change room. She would have to get her street clothes anyway. She passed through the waiting room, where Ara waved at her from a distance and mouthed the words, "Where were you?" Ignoring this, Jenny turned into the hallway that led to the studio.

Jenny's heart sunk as she saw her mother and Kat talking together just outside the change room. Her mother did not look pleased.

The message that Jenny heard repeated over and over on the way home, amidst a lot of angry and disappointed words, was that, as expected, she had taken her last ballet class.

That evening, Ara phoned. Jenny had confined herself to her room since getting home and had refused to come down for dinner, but she decided to take this call in the privacy of her father's office. "So where were you during dance class?" Ara asked.

Jenny told her the entire story, except for the part about setting off the fire alarm. "And the worst part is, my mom found out from Kat that I haven't been dancing in class."

"Oh, my God! So what did she do?"

"She told me I can't take ballet anymore," Jenny replied.

"Oh, my God, that's terrible!" Ara tried to be nice and reassuring, telling Jenny that her parents might change their minds, but Jenny had little hope and couldn't be comforted.

Finally, Ara told Jenny the other reason she had called. "So, I guess you missed hearing Kat and Madame Beaufort talk about this year's recital."

"Yeah," said Jenny. "Why? What happened?"

"It was kind of like they were arguing, except they were talking to the parents instead of each other. And it was kind of like listening to two channels on the TV at the same time. Kat starting talking about improvisation and how we were going to create an original ballet. But Madame kept interrupting, saying they hadn't decided yet, but they were thinking of having us perform an excerpt from either *The Nutcracker* or *Swan Lake*. Then Kat started talking about how everyone would have a unique part to play—which sounded great—and then Madame started talking about how important it was to have the best dancer in the starring role. Both of them were trying to be polite, but Madame kept contradicting everything Kat said until everyone was totally confused. Then the fire alarm went off, and Madame had to turn it off and call the fire department. And after that Madame stood in the corner with her arms folded, shaking her head, while Kat taught the rest of the class herself."

"Wow," said Jenny. "So who won the argument?"

"Well, Madame seemed pretty definite, so I think Kat lost."

After a pause, Ara continued, "But you know what? I've been thinking about what you said. I'm tired of Veronique always being the prima ballerina. I want to see if I can get as good as her by this spring. I have a feeling that with Kat around, some other people might have a chance. And after all, if it's my last year, I may as well go for gold."

"I think you're right," said Jenny. "I think you should be the star. I'd love to see you do it."

"Well, it's not that I want to be a star. I just think it shouldn't be all about Veronique. I'd like to see you dance too, even if not right away. Maybe after your parents have calmed down, they'll give you another chance."

"Maybe," said Jenny. But she didn't really believe it.

After Ara hung up, Jenny began to think. She was angry with her mother for making her quit ballet. And for the past two months, she had felt guilty for deceiving her. Why did learning ballet involve so many bad feelings? Why couldn't she just take part in a dance class and be happy about it like any normal girl?

As she was getting ready for bed that night, Jenny bent down and picked up a pair of pyjamas that had fallen on the floor—without bending her knees. Straightening, she suddenly realized that, two months ago, she couldn't have done that. She looked down at her legs, which had been firmed by hundreds of *relevés*. She had changed in these past two months. And yet, she was just beginning. How much more was there to discover? How much more could she change if she had the chance?

There was something missing in her, a hole that dance promised to fill. It had called to her that first time she saw the DVD of *Swan Lake*, and it was calling even more strongly now.

Jenny decided that, somehow, she had to get back into that studio, and with her parents' blessing next time. She didn't know exactly how to do it. She just knew she would.

Chapter 10
Disaster

The following evening, over dinner, Jenny decided to take the direct approach. "Mom, Dad, I want to go back to ballet class."

Jenny's mother dropped her fork, and it hit the plate with a loud clatter. "You have got to be kidding."

"I'm not. I want to keep going."

Her mother exploded. "No way! After lying to us for months? After we paid for those lessons that you completely shirked? I think you've had all the dance lessons you ever need to take."

"At least I made a friend," Jenny protested.

"That's not the point."

"I thought it was," Jenny muttered under her breath.

For the first time, her father intervened. "Jenny, we're having a hard time understanding this. If you liked ballet, why didn't you participate in class?"

"I liked the class. I love the class. It's my absolute favourite thing in the whole world."

"Then why did you tell your teacher you were too sick to

participate?" her mother protested. "Why didn't you participate? And if you were having problems, why not tell us?"

Jenny hung her head. "It's hard to explain."

"Well, then, don't come to us asking if you can take dance again," her mother said sharply. "You owe us an explanation before asking for more favours."

Jenny breathed in and out a few times, trying to hold her thoughts and feelings together. She could see that she had to try to tell the truth, the whole truth.

"I love ballet. I just get … I'm afraid of dancing in front of everyone. They're all so good."

"Well, there's no point in taking dance lessons if you don't dance." Her mother softened her tone. "Look, Jenny, I think it's important that you choose something else to do after school. Something that wouldn't involve performing, that wouldn't be such a problem for you. Something more practical."

It was now Jenny's turn to explode. "That's all you care about, practical! It's always about how our family is supposed to be trying to get somewhere—make more money."

"You're going to find as you get older, Jenny, that not having money doesn't make for a very happy life. Everyone needs a career these days, girls as well as boys. So why not get a head start on the kind of career you might enjoy?"

"I like ballet."

"Ballet dancers have to dance."

Jenny's anger, now set loose, was proving hard to contain. "You're not listening!" she yelled.

"I am listening," her mother persisted. "But why not choose

something you could actually have fun participating in? Your school has a math and science club."

"I hate math."

"What about a sports team?"

"I hate sports."

"Girl Guides? You could make lots of new friends there."

"You mean Pathfinders."

"Okay, Pathfinders, then."

"I hate Pathfinders."

"You've never tried it!"

"That's because I hate it."

"Why do you hate it?"

"Because it's not ballet!"

"Okay," her father intervened again, "so you like ballet better than anything. But isn't it a little disappointing to just watch while other people have all the fun?"

"I don't just watch," Jenny confessed. "I practise ... at home ... in my room. And I take notes in class, and I make drawings and videos so I can make sure I do it right."

Her mother and father looked at each other, trying to come to terms with this new information.

After a few moments, her mother spoke again. "You know, Jenny, when I was your age, I thought music was the most important thing in my life."

Jenny knew her mom could play piano. But although they owned a keyboard, only her father ever played it. And she certainly had never heard her mother say music was important. "You did?"

Her mother nodded. "I went all through the Royal Conservatory piano grades and started university as a music major. What I really wanted was to be a concert pianist. My teachers all thought I had the potential."

Jenny had never known this about her mother's past. It seemed impossible to imagine her mother—who usually pooh-poohed anything artistic—as a professional musician. "So what happened?"

Her mother took a deep breath. "Stage fright, during my first really important concert. I had been having problems with anxiety for some time. Everyone told me it would get better the more I performed, but instead it got worse. And this time, I was facing a huge crowd—hundreds of people. I was so scared that I almost couldn't face the audience. I finally managed to get to the piano, but I hit a wrong note near the beginning, and I just fell apart. I finished the concert, but that was the last performance I ever gave. I saw a doctor for a time, and he told me I had social phobia—it just means a fear of making a fool of yourself in front of people."

"So what did you do?" Jenny asked.

"I changed my major to accounting. And it was the right choice. Much easier to find work as an accountant than a pianist, especially after we moved to the farm. And after you were born, we needed the income, what with your father's career taking a little time to get established."

Jenny's mother smiled at her husband. "Hey," he said, "that's going to change soon. Teachers make a regular salary too."

"But don't you miss it?" Jenny asked. "The piano, I mean."

"Sometimes," she replied. "Music—well, any art, really—can be very alluring. That's the trouble. If you enjoy it, you start to feel like you can do it too. You don't think about the fact that very few people actually become successful musicians, or painters, or ... even dancers. You find yourself pursuing impossible dreams instead of working toward a career you're actually suited for.

"I'm telling you this because of something the doctor told me back then. He said if one of your parents has social phobia, you're more likely to have it. That's why I want you to make friends, so you get more comfortable with people. I'm worried that you might be like me. And I don't want you to work hard for years at something and then have to give it up."

Jenny toyed with the food on her plate for a moment, pondering what her mother had said. Finally, she replied, "But what if I really can be good at ballet? What if I just need time to, you know, get used to it?"

Her mother shook her head. "Jenny, if you were suited to be a dancer, you would have danced in class. We can't afford to waste money on something that we already know won't happen."

Chapter 11

An Impromptu Journey

Jenny thought about her mother's story over and over that evening, and again the next day at school. By three o'clock, while the rest of her class were trying to finish their math problems before the bell rang—so they wouldn't have homework—Jenny was still gazing into space, twisting her hair, lost in thought.

Her mother had insisted that she was better off—that the family was better off—with her becoming an accountant. But Jenny could only think how sad it was for her mother not to have achieved her big dream.

Could it be true, as her mother had argued, that it's better to pick something you're likely to succeed at, something within your reach? Maybe. But what her mother didn't know was that Jenny had already decided unconsciously, wholeheartedly, that she was a dancer—even if only a secret dancer, even if she only danced on the inside. And that decision was irrevocable.

What would it take, Jenny wondered, to make everything all right? Courage? Maybe. If only she could be more like Ara. Ara would never have this kind of problem. Faced with a scary situation,

Ara would just plunge in and do it. Was it confidence? Audacity? Stupidity? Definitely not stupidity. There was nothing stupid about doing what you loved. Well, whatever Ara had, it worked.

On the other hand, there was Veronique. Veronique's courage seemed to come from effort and control. She worked hard to look as confident and perfect as she did. Jenny could see that every time Veronique danced. And her approach worked too.

And then, there was just plain, everyday courage, like what Trish or Kristen had. It wasn't so much that it completely overcame their self-doubts, but it was enough to let them participate in the classes and performances.

It didn't seem to matter what kind of courage you could muster. Any kind would do, as long as it gave you a way to do what you wanted.

"What you wanted"—maybe that was the clue. Jenny had gone through the whole charade of pretending to be sick and lying to her parents because she wanted to be in that ballet class more than anything. It was her desire that gave her the courage to follow that plan, even if it was a bad plan.

Jenny still wanted to be in ballet class. She wanted it with every fibre of her body. She did not want to lose the opportunity the way her mother had lost hers.

The bell rang. Jenny packed up her books and pen, donned her fall coat, and walked outside with the rest of her classmates. She knew she had to do something to change her situation. She had to find another way to be a part of the dance school. She didn't know what other ways there were, but she had to find one.

As she left the school yard and started to walk home, she passed the place where the city bus stopped. Looking up the street, she could see the bus coming. It was the same bus that also stopped outside the dance school. Jenny put her hand in her coat pocket. There were some coins at the bottom, enough to pay for a ride on the bus.

Without thinking, Jenny ran back to the bus stop, just in time for the bus to stop and open its doors. She climbed on board, dropped the coins in the cash box, and took a seat.

An idea was forming in Jenny's mind. It was Monday, after all. Kat would be teaching the regular Grade Four Ballet class. Jenny needed to be back in that class, and the only person she could think of who might help her find a way was Kat. Not Madame Beaufort. She wouldn't be sympathetic. But Jenny had a feeling Kat might.

It was only a twenty-minute ride to the Kingston Ballet School. Jenny got off the bus outside the school well before the start of ballet class. She didn't really know what she would say or do or ask for. But she summoned up her courage and walked up the steps and into the building.

There was only one person in the waiting room. Robyn was slouched on a sofa, staring at the ceiling. Her red hair, tied in a loose ponytail, was splayed over the sofa cushion behind her head. She looked completely bored.

"Hi," said Robyn, as she rolled her eyes down to look at Jenny. "I thought you weren't coming anymore."

"I'm not ... at least, I'm not sure," said Jenny. "Is Kat here?"

"With Mom and Veronique in the studio. You'll have to sit and wait. Veronique's getting a private lesson."

"A private lesson?" Jenny hadn't known you could have private lessons in ballet. *Maybe ...,* she thought. But no, her mother would never go for it. It would be way too expensive.

Jenny sat on the couch next to Robyn.

"Yeah, you know Veronique." Robyn rolled her eyes. "She's decided her mission in life is to head off to Toronto to be a star, and Mom wants her to as well. Stupid ballet."

"Why do you say it's stupid?" Jenny asked.

"Well, I guess it's okay if it's what you want to do."

"Don't you?"

Robyn sat up a little. "I guess I can tell you since you're not in ballet anymore. You know this is only my first year dancing, right?"

Jenny hadn't known this, but she nodded anyway.

Robyn continued. "See, for the past five years, I was taking kung fu. That's what I really like. I was good at it too. I came close to winning the regional championship last year. Now I have to do this instead."

"How come?"

A trace of a smile played on Robyn's face. Jenny couldn't quite tell if it was pride or embarrassment. "'Cause I got into a little fight at school. It wasn't my fault. This kid was picking on some little kids, and he wouldn't quit, so I told him off ... and things got out of hand. After that, my dad and stepmom decided I should take up a more 'ladylike' activity."

"But you don't like dance?"

"It's okay. I'm just not sure what the point of it is. I mean, when in real life do you need to pirouette? Besides, you should be able to do what you like, what you're good at, shouldn't you? I mean, if you feel like there's something you're meant to do, you should do it, right? You shouldn't be forced to do something else."

"No," Jenny agreed. "You shouldn't."

At that moment, Madame Beaufort, Kat, and Veronique came into the room.

"Jenny?" Madame Beaufort looked surprised. "We weren't expecting you here today."

"Please," said Jenny, "I need to speak to Kat, I mean, Miss Miles."

"We can go into the office," Kat suggested.

Kat led Jenny into the ballet school office and offered her a chair. Kat sat down behind the desk.

"Before you tell me why you're here," said Kat, "I have to ask you something." She looked Jenny firmly in her eye. "Do your parents know where you are?"

"No," Jenny admitted.

"You came on your own?"

Jenny nodded.

"Okay, well, I think we should phone them and let them know you're here. Then we can talk."

Jenny nodded again. She watched while Kat looked up Jenny's phone number and tapped it out on the phone.

Only now did Jenny begin to think about the fact that she was probably in trouble again. Kat didn't look angry, but Jenny really didn't know what she could realistically ask for. What did she want to do? Ask to join the class again for free? That didn't seem likely. As Kat spoke to Jenny's mother on the phone, Jenny felt more and more that the situation was hopeless.

Finally, Kat hung up. "Your parents are on their way to pick you up," she informed Jenny. "That gives us a few minutes to talk before they get here. So tell me, what's so important that you came to see me rather than go straight home after school?"

Jenny didn't know where to start. What she really wanted seemed so pointless to ask for. And then, she noticed the pink Bristol board, leaning on its side against the back of a shelf, behind Kat's left shoulder. It was the one that used to be in the waiting room, the one that read, "Volunteers Wanted."

"I want to be a volunteer," Jenny said.

Chapter 12
An Outrageous Proposal

Kat blinked. "A volunteer?"

"I want to volunteer in the school. I want to be able to sit in the dance classes and watch, same as before, even if I'm not actually part of the class. I'll do anything in return—run the CD player, sweep the studio, whatever you need done."

Kat frowned, thinking. "When we put up the notice asking for volunteers, we meant parent volunteers. The school needs parents who can help raise money, or make costumes, or help backstage at performances. We've never had student volunteers. Why would you think of that?"

"I want to be a dancer."

"Really?" Kat looked doubtful.

"I do," Jenny insisted. "I know I haven't been dancing in class, but I love ballet. And even if I can't do it, I want to be a part of it. I want to see how it's done. I want to learn everything about it. Please, you're my only hope. My parents won't let me take lessons anymore. And I have to find another way."

Kat sat silent for a minute, considering. "Jenny, you know I can't agree to anything that would go against your parents' wishes."

"I know, but this wouldn't actually be 'taking ballet.' And if you could help me convince them …"

"Let me talk to Madame Beaufort about it," Kat conceded. "Just wait here for me."

Kat stood up and left the room. Jenny waited a moment and then looked out the door, to the waiting room. Robyn and Veronique were sitting on the couch, talking. Kat and Madame Beaufort were at the far end of the room, speaking in low voices. Kat had her back to Jenny. Madame Beaufort did not have a very kindly look on her face.

Jenny wondered what they were saying to each other. Were they angry? Were they trying to think of some nice way to get rid of her? Their conversation went on and on.

Jenny heard her mother and father arrive while the two teachers were still talking. She immediately turned her back to the doorway and moved to where she thought they couldn't see her. She heard Kat say hello to them. A moment later, Kat escorted them into the office. Madame Beaufort followed.

"Jenny!" Her mother's voice betrayed her anxiety. "What in the world were you thinking?" She immediately threw her arms around Jenny, while Jenny's father put one hand on his wife's shoulder and the other on his daughter's. "Don't you know how worried we were when you didn't come home?"

"I'm sorry," Jenny said.

"What are you doing here?" her father asked.

Jenny shrugged. She didn't know what to say. She felt badly for making her mother upset.

Kat cleared her throat. "May I say something?"

Jenny's mother reluctantly turned her eyes from Jenny to look at Kat.

"Jenny came here today to see me," Kat continued. "Unexpectedly," she added.

Madame Beaufort added, "Naturally, we don't condone such behaviour from our students ... or ex-students."

"Naturally," Kat agreed. "But I think you ought to know the reason. Jenny came to ask for a volunteer position at the school."

"What?" Jenny's mother was taken aback.

"I told her she would need your approval first and that under no circumstances should she be coming here without permission. But Madame Beaufort and I have discussed it, and we think we could do with Jenny's help."

"That is," Madame Beaufort corrected, "Katrina feels that Jenny, despite appearances, may have a passion for the ballet, which she is willing to encourage."

Jenny's heart soared. Maybe they did want her.

Jenny's mom looked at her. "We've already discussed this."

"Please, Mom," Jenny begged.

Jenny's mother seemed confused. She looked at Kat. "I don't understand. What exactly would she be volunteering to do?"

"I taught at another school where we had older students help out with the younger classes," Kat said. "High school students, for instance, get credit these days for community service and volunteer work. It's never been done at this school because we haven't yet had classes for adolescents."

"We have been expanding the school gradually, beginning with the younger grades," Madame Beaufort explained.

"But Jenny is old enough that she could be a help to us," Kat concluded.

"You expect Jenny to teach the younger students?" her mother asked incredulously.

"I said help, not teach," said Kat. "It would be a way for her to learn through exposure and to give something in return.

Jenny's mother looked at Jenny and then at her husband, who said, "Obviously, we will need to discuss this before making any decisions."

"I understand," said Kat. "Just give me a call once you've made up your mind."

Once she and her parents were in the car, on their way home, Jenny asked, "Please, can I volunteer?"

Her mother looked back over the front seat and began to say what was really on her mind. "We should ground you for a month for this stunt. How dare you go so far from home without telling us."

"I'm sorry," Jenny said. "I didn't know what else to do."

"That doesn't matter. What's gotten into you these past few months? You never used to be so irresponsible. You never used to lie to us. You worry me."

"I'm sorry," Jenny said.

"Are you angry with us over something? Is this your way of getting back at us for taking you to a new home and school?"

"No."

"Then what is it?"

Jenny reflected for a moment, trying to sort out her feelings. "Nothing ever mattered so much before."

Her mother turned to her father, who was driving, and asked, "What do you think about this?"

He was silent for a moment and then asked Jenny, "Is being in that ballet class really worth all this?"

"Yes," said Jenny.

"Worth lying to us and to your teachers all those weeks?"

Jenny felt guilty. But her honest answer was still yes.

"Worth what you did today?"

"Yes."

"Worth doing whatever work they ask you to do as a volunteer?"

"Yes," said Jenny, a glimmer of hope now beginning to stir in her.

"Even though it will still be everyone else and not you who gets to perform on stage?"

"Yes."

Her father glanced at her mother. "I hate to say it, but I think we have an artist in the making."

But her mother was not yet satisfied. When the Sparks sat down to dinner that evening, she raised the subject again. "I've thought about this volunteering idea some more, and I don't think it will be a productive use of Jenny's time."

"Mom!" Jenny wailed.

"Why do you say that?" asked her father.

"Well, where's it going to lead? It will take up her after-school time, which means her homework and grades will suffer. And yet, what will she get out of it? Will she gain a practical skill? Will she make friends? Will it lead to something in the future?"

"She might learn responsibility," her father suggested. "The fact that she seems to want this so badly ... I mean, if she is willing to go to such lengths just to be part of that school, surely that much dedication will lead somewhere."

"Yes, to a dead end."

Her father shrugged. "I think it's worth finding out where it will lead. What if she has some talent we don't know about? We might crush it if we don't let her use this opportunity."

Jenny's mother thought about this for a moment and then looked back at her. "If we agree to let you do this, it will only be on two conditions."

Jenny could feel hope well up inside her. Her mother sounded like she might give in.

"First," her mother continued, "that your grades at school don't suffer."

Jenny practically leaped out of her chair with excitement. They were going to let her do it. "I promise," she said.

"And second, I want to see some sign by the end of the year that this volunteer work is worthwhile."

Jenny found this second requirement a little confusing. "What do you mean 'worthwhile'?"

"I want some sign that it's worth all the extra effort you're going to put in. I'm not convinced it will be. In fact, I'm pretty sure it won't. But I'm willing to let you have until the end of this school year to prove me wrong. Or at least get ballet out of your system."

Jenny frowned. "But what sort of sign do you want?"

"I'm not sure. That's up to you to come up with. Or maybe it will happen on its own. But if, by the end of the year, there's no proof that volunteering has been worthwhile, then I want you to pick a different after-school activity next year." She looked at Jenny's father. "What do you think?"

"I think that's fair," he said. Then he turned to his daughter. "Jenny?"

"Yes! I mean, I don't know exactly what I can do. But yes. Thanks, Mom. Thanks, Dad. Will you call Kat right now to let her know?"

"The school will be closed now," said her father. "We'll phone tomorrow."

That night, Jenny went to bed happier than she had been in a very long time. Everything felt like it was finally falling into place.

Chapter 13

A Willing Volunteer

Jenny's mother phoned Kat the next day and arranged for Jenny to begin her volunteer job at the school. They decided that Jenny would help out at the Saturday morning Pre-Ballet and Beginning Ballet classes, which were taught to five-, six-, and seven-year-olds. In return, she could observe other classes, including the Grade Four Ballet class in which she had previously been a student.

Jenny was ecstatic when she heard that it was all arranged. All the pressure, all the anxiety she had felt for months vanished instantly. She could attend more ballet classes than ever, without having to dance in any of them. She would be part of the school, without costing her parents money. It was perfect.

Once her initial excitement had faded, however, Jenny realized that she needed to make the most of this opportunity. Her mother didn't think this plan would be worthwhile. She thought Jenny would be better off doing something else. Well, Jenny was determined to show her she was wrong.

For the rest of that week, Jenny was extra scrupulous about finishing her homework quickly and perfectly. She even read as far ahead in her textbooks as she could, to make sure she wouldn't fall behind later.

Jenny did her ballet exercises in her room each night, now without the fear of being discovered. She also asked her father to take out as many books on ballet as he could from the university library. The more she knew about ballet, Jenny thought, the more of a help she could be as a volunteer. But that wasn't the real reason.

The truth was that Jenny was already hatching another secret plan. Her mother wanted a sign. And Jenny wanted to give her one. Jenny felt that if she could learn everything there was to know about ballet and if she practised hard on her own until she could do all the steps perfectly, then maybe she could eventually be confident enough to participate in a class. And if she could participate in a class, even just once, maybe her mother would take that as a sign and let her go on volunteering.

Kat had asked if Jenny could arrive early for her first day of volunteering so she would have time to learn what her new job would involve. So Saturday morning, Jenny's father dropped her at the dance school promptly at nine o'clock.

Even though she was sure no one expected her to dance, Jenny nonetheless changed into her leotard, tights, and slippers. Somehow, they made her feel more professional.

Jenny found Kat in the studio, sorting through a pile of CDs that were stacked on top of the piano.

"Good morning, Jenny," Kat called out. "Can I ask you a favour? Could you find my stool? Someone seems to have moved it."

Jenny turned around and walked back to the waiting room. She poked her head in the office and found the stool behind the desk, next to the office chair. She picked it up and carried it back to the studio.

"Great," said Kat when she saw the stool. Jenny set it down next to the piano, and Kat eased herself onto it.

"Now let's talk about Pre-Ballet," Kat began. "At this level, the students are too young to do any real dance training. It wouldn't be good for their bodies. So they learn first and second positions only, *demi-plié*, a few simple stretches, rhythm games, some simple steps like skipping, marching, and jumping, and some imaginative movement—improvisation. The third class this morning is Beginner Ballet. That's for seven-year-olds. Because they're slightly older, they learn *rélevé, battement tendu, piqué,* and a few other simple steps— nothing you haven't seen before."

Jenny was already starting to feel a fluttering in her stomach. "What do you want me to do?" she asked.

"Well," said Kat, "basically, you can help me by setting an example—doing the exercises along with the students, helping me keep them focused. Later on, I may get you to help me check their posture. We want them to develop good habits at this age—no swayback or sickle foot. By next week, you'll know them by name, so you can take attendance for me. There may be other things too. We'll just have to see how it goes."

Kat paused. "How does that sound? Think you can do it?"

"Okay," said Jenny, although she didn't feel very confident about demonstrating.

"You'll do fine," Kat reassured her. "Once you see these kids, you'll see there's nothing to be nervous about. Any questions?"

"Doesn't Madame Beaufort teach today?" Jenny asked.

"Oh, she comes in later to teach the older classes: Grades One to Four. I teach Pre- and Beginner Ballet since they're new this year, and they were my idea. Kids who start young often continue, so hopefully these classes will increase enrolment for next year. Besides, I need to earn a living. And right now, apart from these classes, I'm only doing the advanced work with the Grade Four classes and some private lessons."

There was something Jenny had been curious about for some time, and now seemed the perfect opportunity. "Can I ask you something?" she said.

"Sure," said Kat.

"Why did you stop dancing with the National Ballet? I mean, why come …?"

"To this little school?" Kat gave a painful smile. "Car accident. Last year. The doctors told me I shouldn't dance anymore—at least not at the same level as before."

"That's terrible!" Jenny exclaimed.

Kat shrugged and smiled. "A dancer's career always ends sooner than she'd like. I'm just glad I studied teaching as well as performing. I've been taking physiotherapy and Pilates classes, so I'm much better than I was. In a few months, I'm hoping I'll be able to do most things without much pain. After that, I have high hopes for this school."

It wasn't long before the Pre-Ballet students began arriving. There were seven of them—all girls. As they came through the door, Jenny made an important discovery. The students were all so little. Somehow, it hadn't sunk in before what "five years old" really meant. But when Jenny saw them, she realized how completely unintimidating they were. She felt more inclined to hug them than run and hide. Kat introduced her, and she spent a few minutes helping some of the girls tie the strings or elastics on their ballet slippers and getting to know their names. When Kat began teaching, Jenny found that the exercises were so simple, she didn't mind demonstrating at all.

Twenty minutes into the forty-five minute class, Jenny was given another task. Half the girls suddenly decided they needed to go to the washroom. The rest wanted a drink of water. And because the washrooms were at the other end of the building, they needed an escort. So Jenny took them.

Imaginative movement occupied the last few minutes of class. Really, it was much like improvisation but with a little more guidance. Kat had Jenny put some music on the stereo. Then she invited the students to pretend to be different things—animals, forces of nature, and the like. She made up a story as she went along. As Kat led the movements, Jenny switched CD tracks when asked.

By the time the second class began—for six-year-olds—Jenny was feeling much more relaxed. She found she was able to offer encouragement to the students when it was needed. Once they had been introduced, the girls actually seemed to look up to her.

After Pre-Ballet came Beginner Ballet. These kids were seven years old, but the format of the class was much the same. The exercises were only slightly more advanced. By now, Jenny had thoroughly warmed up to her job, and her anxiety had almost disappeared.

When the morning classes had ended and the Beginner Ballet students had left with their parents, Kat said to Jenny, "Good job today. You seem to have a knack for working with younger kids."

"Thanks," said Jenny. In fact, she had really enjoyed herself.

"You've been doing some training on your own, haven't you?" Kat asked.

Jenny was taken aback. "How did you know?"

"I can tell by your muscle tone in certain places and by watching you do some of the movements this morning. Would you mind if I gave you a few corrections sometime? Just so you don't develop poor habits either?"

"No," said Jenny. "That would be great."

"Okay," Kat said. "Next Saturday morning before classes, we'll grab a few minutes. Right now, I have to give a private lesson. You can go eat lunch if you like, or stay and watch."

Jenny could never pass on the opportunity to watch a ballet class, so she decided to stay and watch. Once again, the private lesson turned out to be for Veronique's benefit. Kat, apparently, had been recruited to help Veronique bring her technical skills to even greater heights. By listening carefully, Jenny learned that Veronique had passed her audition—the first round anyway. If she passed the next round, she would be into next summer's dance program at the National Ballet School in Toronto. And if that went well, she would be accepted into the full-time program in the fall. These extra lessons were to give her an edge.

Jenny stayed out of the way while the private lesson was happening, skulking in her usual spot by the piano. But she watched everything Kat taught carefully. She resolved to bring her notebook next week.

The Grade Four Ballet class had recently been switched to one thirty to make room in the schedule for Beginning Ballet. Jenny felt a little nervous about seeing everyone again. But at least she didn't have to pretend anything anymore. Ara, in particular, seemed glad to see her. When the class ended and Jenny went to change back into her street clothes, Ara plied her with questions.

"How come you're back? Did your parents change their minds?"

Jenny explained about her new volunteer job. The other girls listened as they changed.

"Wow," said Ara. "So what do you do as a volunteer?"

"Anything I can to help out," Jenny replied.

Veronique, who had been listening along with the other girls, picked up an empty juice can and chip bag (the remains of a preclass snack) and walked over to Jenny. "Good," she said. "We could use a helper." Then she smiled sweetly, handed Jenny her garbage, and said, "Would you mind throwing these out for me?"

Jenny felt a momentary confusion. She didn't think this was part of her job description, but she didn't want to look uncooperative either. So she said, "Sure," and took the garbage out to the wastebasket in the waiting room.

Jenny returned to the change room just as Ara was leaving. She pulled Ara aside and whispered to her, "Did you know Kat is giving Veronique private lessons?"

From the way Ara's eyes widened, Jenny could tell this was news. "We really need to talk," said Ara. "I'll phone you tonight, okay?"

That evening, when Jenny answered the phone, Ara began asking her questions. "You still want to dance, right?"

"Yes," said Jenny.

"But you're too nervous to dance in class, right?"

Jenny thought for a moment. Today she had done more than ever before, but the thought of participating in a class with girls her own age still seemed like an insurmountable challenge. "Right," she said.

"But you've been practising on your own, right?"

"Right."

"Okay, I've got an idea. Remember me saying that I think some other people should have a chance to have solo parts in this year's recital? Because it's getting really boring with Veronique always being centre stage."

"Yeah," said Jenny. "And you said you wanted to give her some competition."

"Oh, did I? Well, yeah. I've decided I want to see if I can improve so much that they'll have to give me a bigger part, and maybe some other people too. But if Veronique's getting private lessons, then how can I compete? The only way for me to get as good as her would be to get some private lessons myself. But my parents aren't going to pay for me to have private lessons, so I have to get some on my own. See what I mean?"

"Yes," said Jenny. "But how?"

"Well, I was thinking that, actually, we both need private lessons. I need lessons to get good enough to outdance Veronique, and you need lessons on becoming less nervous so you can dance at all—or at least take classes. So I was thinking, why don't we train each other?"

Jenny was taken aback. "But how could we train each other? I don't know enough about ballet to teach anyone."

"Maybe not, but I bet you could help me anyway. You're smart. You notice things. All you have to do is watch me and figure out what I need to do to dance better than Veronique. I can't really watch myself—I've tried. It's like I know all the things I'm supposed to do, but when I dance I just get carried away with the feeling. It feels great while I'm doing it, but then Madame Beaufort tells me I'm not using proper technique. But you know how to do it because you watch yourself all the time, don't you? You worry about what everyone thinks of you, right?"

"Right," said Jenny.

"Besides, now that you have the chance to see what goes on in Veronique's private lessons, you can tell me so I can practise the same things."

It was a wild idea, and there were some things that went on in the private lessons that Kat probably wouldn't want Jenny to share. On the other hand, Jenny wanted to help Ara. "Okay, maybe I could do that," she said.

"And then, maybe I can help you loosen up and get dancing. I mean, I don't really understand what it's like to be you, but I know what it's like to be me, so maybe I can help you be more—" Ara paused, searching for the right word.

"Flamboyant?" Jenny suggested.

"Hmm," said Ara. "Flamboyant. Yeah, that's what you need to be."

"Sounds like a long shot," said Jenny. But inside she felt a glimmer of hope stirring. After all, if she was ever to be a dancer, she had to start sometime. Maybe all she needed was an atmosphere that felt less intimidating—like with the Pre-Ballet class this morning. Jenny was pretty sure Ara wouldn't make fun of her or criticize her. So maybe, if it was just the two of them, that would be a small step forward.

"Well, maybe it is a long shot," Ara admitted, "but what have we got to lose?"

Chapter 14

The Point of *Pointe*

Jenny and Ara arranged to meet at Ara's house after school the following Tuesday and cleared it with their parents. Although the girls went to different schools, Ara's house was close enough for Jenny to walk to.

Standing outside Ara's front door, Jenny felt suddenly tempted to turn around and leave. A part of her still didn't want to dance in front of anyone, even Ara. But she steeled herself and pushed the doorbell button. This could be, after all, the best chance she would ever have.

When Ara answered the door, she was already wearing her leotard and tights. "Did you bring your dance gear to change into?" she asked.

"I did," Jenny confessed, pulling her dance bag into better view. "I wasn't sure if I should, since it's not a real class. But it makes me feel more like a dancer."

"Well, that is the idea," said Ara. "So let's do it. You can change in my room. But let's not worry about hair. I get so tired of putting it up."

A few minutes later, Jenny returned to the main floor, suitably dressed for ballet. Ara led her downstairs to the basement rec room. It was the only room in the house big enough to practise in. Ara explained that she had had a lengthy shouting match with her brothers and sister that morning to establish that the rec room would be off-limits when Jenny came over. The two girls rolled back the large area rug to expose the tile floor underneath.

"This floor's not sprung, like the studio," Ara explained, "but it's smooth enough to dance on and not too slippery."

"What do you mean 'sprung'?" Jenny asked.

"Oh, didn't you know? The studio has a special floor. It's bouncier, so it's easier on the feet."

"Is that why it's a few inches higher than the hallway?"

"I think so. Anyway, this floor will do for today."

"It's better than my basement," Jenny agreed. "Mine's just concrete."

There was no barre, but Ara pointed to a small bookcase along one wall that was roughly the height of Jenny's waist. "You can use this as a barre when we get to that part. It's sturdy enough."

Jenny looked at the bookcase. It wasn't long enough for both of them to use without bumping into each other. "What about you?"

"I thought I'd try practising without a barre." Ara tilted her head, shrugging slightly. "I've had more ballet classes, and my legs are pretty strong already." Having closely observed all the girls in their class for months, Jenny knew this was true. Ara's leg muscles were exceptionally well toned.

Jenny was already feeling nervous.

"Okay," Ara began, "I was thinking we should start off getting you dancing. Then we can spend a little time on the harder stuff. We should probably start with a basic warm-up, just like in class. Then maybe just a short review, just to get you used to it." She tapped her chin. "What did we do last class?"

Jenny pulled her notebook out of her dance bag. Opening it, she said, "Name the date, and I can tell you exactly what the class did."

"Wow," Ara said, looking at Jenny's detailed notes. "Maybe you should pick the warm-up."

"Okay," said Jenny, and she flipped to the page of the book where she had made her most recent entry.

Just before they began, Jenny said, "Promise you won't laugh at me?"

"I'll make you a deal," said Ara, extending her hand. "Anytime you feel stupid, let me know, and I'll do something twice as stupid so you can laugh at me."

Jenny shook Ara's hand and laughed. "Deal."

They began their warm-up. Jenny felt very self-conscious at first. But somehow, she knew Ara wouldn't think worse of her no matter what mistakes she made. Not that she made any. After months of practising on her own, she had most of the exercises down pat.

After a few stretches on the floor, the girls moved on to barre work (or in Jenny's case, shelf work). "You know," Ara said, in the middle of a *battement tendu*, "You really have nothing to worry about. You're a great dancer."

"You're just trying to make me feel better," said Jenny.

"No, really, you are!" Ara insisted.

"Thanks. It is a lot easier here than in a group." It was easier, Jenny found, except for when it came to dancing across the floor. In class, students usually did this one at time, so each dancer had lots of space to move through. Jenny, however, couldn't bring herself to dance by herself with Ara standing aside watching her, so they crossed the floor side by side, at the same time.

"Face it," said Ara, after they had gone through almost all the exercises from the last class and had collapsed onto a couch for a short rest, "you can dance. You just worry too much."

"I can't help it," Jenny said. "I just get nervous with anyone watching—well, anyone our age or older."

"Ah, don't worry." Ara made a dismissive wave with her hand. "A few more practices and I bet you won't care how big the audience is."

Jenny was unconvinced but didn't argue. "Let's do you now," she said.

"Okay." Ara jumped up. "Here's the thing. Remember that sequence we did at the end of last class? Madame Beaufort praised Veronique, as usual, and then told me I need to pay more attention to what I'm doing."

"I remember," said Jenny, as the memory of it flashed across her brain.

"Okay, so this is how it went." Ara ran to one corner of the room. Then she danced the sequence as she remembered it. "Now what was wrong with that?"

Jenny thought for a moment, trying to picture in her mind how Veronique did it, how Madame Beaufort had looked when demonstrating. "It's not that you're doing anything wrong. It's just that Veronique is so much more precise. It's like she prepares for each step ahead of time, so her balance is better. You tend to let yourself get a little off balance, and you use that energy to throw yourself a little too far into the next movement."

Ara thought about this for a moment. "But that's what makes ballet fun."

"Well, maybe," Jenny said, hoping she didn't sound too critical. "But it makes you look less graceful. At least, less than Veronique."

Ara shrugged. "Okay, so what should I do?"

"What if you tried doing it slower?" Jenny suggested.

"Slower?"

"You know, like that day when Kat put the metronome on and you had to improvise at different speeds."

"How could I forget?" Ara raised an eyebrow.

"Well, yeah. But Veronique's not here now to bang into you. What if you just imagined that we had a metronome set on slow ... or maybe I could clap slowly? Then try to do the sequence as exactly as possible, planning each step ahead of time."

Ara shrugged again. "I'll try it."

"Okay. So just do the same sequence again, and if you come to the end, just repeat it."

Jenny began clapping out a slow rhythm, not super slow, but slower than Ara usually liked to move. "More exact," she called out. "Think about being balanced every step of the way. Think about where you're going and what muscles you'll need to use next."

Jenny slowed the rhythm to an unnatural crawl. Ara had to struggle to move slowly enough without falling over, on top of her effort to do the steps correctly. She looked a bit like a fly trying to escape from a spiderweb.

After Ara practised the sequence a few times at this slow crawl, she began to look more comfortable with it. So Jenny started speeding up the rhythm of her clapping to a more normal pace. "Now see if you can keep it precise as you go faster," Jenny instructed.

And for a moment, it seemed to work. Ara was dancing with a level of control and precision Jenny had never seen her use before. When Jenny stopped clapping, she said, "That was great!"

Ara frowned. "It was horrible."

"No, really, it looked much better—almost as good as Veronique."

"No, I mean it's horrible trying to dance that way," Ara said. "I lose the happy feeling when I have to concentrate so hard."

"Well, maybe that's just because you haven't done it this way before," Jenny suggested. "Maybe it just takes practice."

"Maybe," said Ara, though she sounded a little reluctant. "Did it really look better?"

"Yes, it did," Jenny replied.

"Well, I guess it's worth practising," Ara conceded, "if it means a shot at a solo part."

From that day on, Jenny went to Ara's house every Tuesday, Wednesday, and Friday so they could practise ballet together. Usually, Mrs. Reyes would invite Jenny to stay to dinner, and Jenny often accepted. Much as she liked the quiet of her own home and parents, she found she also enjoyed being around the noise and laughter of a bigger family.

On Saturdays, Mondays, and Thursdays, Jenny and Ara both attended the Grade Four Ballet class. Jenny observed each lesson and took detailed notes.

Meanwhile, Jenny's volunteer work on Saturday mornings continued. She enjoyed working with the younger kids each week, and Kat seemed to appreciate her help as well.

Unfortunately, it wasn't all fun. Sometimes Kat asked Jenny to do dull jobs, like stuffing envelopes or photocopying or making sure the rosin pan in the studio was filled. Once, Madame Beaufort asked her to mop the waiting room floor, after a particularly rainy day caused all the parents to leave muddy shoe prints.

What Jenny especially disliked was that Veronique seemed to have decided that part of Jenny's job was to be her personal assistant. During her private lessons, she often asked Jenny to do little favours for her, such as running to the change room to fetch her water bottle or an extra bunpin. While she was always polite, Jenny felt that Veronique secretly enjoyed treating her like a servant.

While none of the other girls in the Grade Four class asked her to do things for them, Jenny worried that they now looked down on her, as if she were a failed dancer who had become the Cinderella of the school.

Not that Jenny spoke to them very much. In fact, apart from Ara, the only person who did talk to her regularly was Robyn, who seemed to think that Jenny had found a clever way to get out of dance class, one that she wished she had thought of herself. Jenny didn't have it in her to explain that she loved dance as much as any of the students. It would have made her Saturdays lonelier.

What made everything bearable was the fun Jenny had in her practise sessions with Ara. The two were becoming best friends.

Gradually, Jenny became more comfortable dancing alongside Ara, as long as Ara didn't look directly at her while she was moving. Improvisation was still out of the question, but she became more relaxed about doing warm-ups, barre work, and even adagios together. Ara continually encouraged Jenny to become less self-conscious, to perform the movements without worrying about making mistakes.

Jenny, in turn, encouraged Ara to pay closer attention to each step and to avoid mistakes. She had decided it was her mission in life to make Ara a better dancer than Veronique. Whenever Ara became carried away with her own enjoyment and enthusiasm, Jenny would remind her to slow down, to use more control over her movements, and to pay attention to what every part of her body was doing and how it was placed.

Jenny felt pleased as she saw Ara's dancing gradually improve. Unfortunately, Veronique was also getting more skillful, thanks in part to her private lessons. Consequently, she still received the bulk of praise (and attention) in class. Of course, it was not too surprising that Madame Beaufort was biased toward her own daughter. But even Kat, who was generally pretty fair, seemed to comment on Veronique's skill far more than Ara's.

One Wednesday, in Ara's basement, while Jenny was coaching her through a difficult sequence, Ara's frustration exploded out of her. "I don't understand why this isn't working!" she suddenly screamed. "I think I'm getting better. You think I'm getting better. So why don't Kat and Madame seem to notice? Why does everyone still think Veronique is God's gift to dance?"

Jenny frowned, thinking. She wanted very much to help Ara and was feeling frustrated herself. "I don't know. Maybe they still remember the accident. Maybe they're afraid to tell you how well you're doing in case it goes to your head."

Ara wasn't really listening. Her mind was still consumed with frustration. "And you know what the worst part is? Dancing this way isn't as much fun!"

"What do you mean?"

"I mean, trying to make everything exact and doing it the same way each time takes the fun out of it. I miss just following my feelings."

Jenny tried to digest this. She had a very clear picture in her mind of the differences between Ara's style and Veronique's. Ara, when she danced her way, was all spontaneity and surprise. She excelled at *allegro*—fast movements that she could throw herself into (sometimes a little too literally). She was as fluid and thrilling to watch as the otters Jenny used to see playing along the frozen shore of the lake by her old home. Veronique, on the other hand, danced with the mechanical precision of a music box doll. Her strength lay in adagio, slow, precise, graceful movements that required intense concentration, strength, and balance. Both girls were great in their own way.

So far, Jenny had focused on helping Ara develop Veronique's level of precision and control. But if Ara lost the enthusiasm that made her great, would she be better or worse in the end? How could one dancer become like the other without losing the thing that made her great on her own?

All of the sudden, an image popped into Jenny's head. "Have you ever tried imitating Veronique?"

"You mean I should dance like her? I thought that was what this was all about."

"No," said Jenny, "not dance like her. Imitate her. You know, um …" she struggled to find the words "like you were doing a dance in order to show everyone why they should not be like her."

Ara's face brightened at the idea. "Oh, you mean like this?" Ara marched across the floor doing an imitation of a ballet-dancing robot, her body and face unnaturally stiff, eyes crossed.

Jenny laughed. "Well, not the eyes. But that's the idea. Try to do the sequence like you were Veronique times two, just for fun."

Ara danced the sequence again, stiffly but precisely. It wasn't exactly beautiful, but it was more controlled.

"You know what," said Jenny, "in a strange way, that was better."

"No way!" Ara protested. "I can't dance like that. It's like wearing a body cast. It's like trying to swim in a ski jacket."

"That's okay," said Jenny. She knew they were on the right track. She could feel a solution about to break out. "Try it one more time, but this time, do it like you were this beautiful bird that someone imprisoned inside a body cast, so you can only move the way the cast will let you. But at the same time you're trying to break free of the body cast, like you are trying to push beyond the body cast into the freedom and joy you're longing for."

Ara took a second to conjure up the image in her own head. Then she launched herself into the sequence again.

The transformation was astounding. Ara, at least in Jenny's opinion, was dancing better than she ever had in class. It was beautiful, passionate, and controlled at the same time. Jenny's eyes widened in surprise and wonder as she watched.

"That was incredible!" Jenny said when Ara finished.

"Really?" said Ara, doubtfully.

"Really! You should have seen yourself. It was better than anything either you or Veronique have ever done!"

Ara digested this for a moment and then said, "Let's do some more!"

For the next hour, Ara practised every dance sequence she could think of in what she decided to call her "new style," while Jenny coached from the sidelines.

Finally, Mrs. Reyes called down to them that dinner was almost ready.

"You know," said Ara, when they had gone up to her room to change. "I just realized something. All this time, I never wanted to dance like Veronique. I always thought it was so unfair that she got all the big roles dancing the way she does. I always tried to be different, more like how I thought ballet should be. I think I liked being different. It doesn't feel too great to think that might have actually held me back."

"That's not what held you back," Jenny reassured her. "Maybe it's just that, while she was developing control, you were developing passion. You both became good at different things. But now, you can add the control to what you have and be better than ever. I bet it's easier to add control when you have passion than to develop passion when all you have is control."

"I hope so," said Ara.

"Trust me. Remember, I've seen what goes on in Veronique's private lessons. Passion is something she hasn't got a clue about."

Ara laughed. Then she drew in a fast breath, as though she had just remembered something important. "You haven't told me what Veronique is working on in those private lessons!"

Jenny hesitated before telling Ara, "Kat has been working on two things with Veronique. Improvisation, which she sucks at, and … pointe work."

Ara screamed. "She's going en pointe! You've got to tell me how, what they're doing, every detail. If Veronique goes en pointe, then I have to too!"

"But it's dangerous," Jenny protested. "Kat says you need to be taught properly, by a real teacher."

"I don't have a choice. You have to tell me everything she does, every tip Kat gives her, and share them with me."

"But what if you hurt yourself? What if I get something wrong and you get some fatal flaw in your technique?"

"It's a chance I have to take," Ara insisted. "If Veronique's the only one who can dance en pointe, then she'll automatically get the solo again. Nothing I do will make any difference."

Jenny could see Ara's point. She knew how much it meant to Ara to get ahead, to have the chance to win the scholarship for next year. Ara had to continue doing the thing she loved, the thing she was obviously born to do. But Jenny could also see Kat's point. What if, by trying to get ahead, Ara hurt herself so badly that she had to quit dance altogether? Would it be Jenny's fault?

Jenny looked straight into Ara's eyes for a moment. Somehow, in that instant, she had a feeling that despite her reputation for recklessness, Ara wouldn't do anything really crazy. Somehow, Ara would know where to draw the line.

"Okay," said Jenny. "But you'll need to get a pair of pointe shoes."

Chapter 15

Dancing in the Dark

From that day on, Ara became practically obsessed with training as hard as she could. Jenny showed Ara the preliminary exercises Kat had taught Veronique. These were designed to strengthen her feet and toes before she started actual pointe work.

At the same time, Jenny kept prodding Ara to combine control with passion in her dancing. Ara found it hard to do consistently. She had to fight the urge to return to her old habits. But she put up with Jenny's reminders for the sake of becoming a better dancer.

In return, however, Ara made one condition. She insisted that Jenny had to keep coming up with new routines for her to do. "It's just too boring," she explained, "to do the same steps the same way over and over. If I have to dance with precision, then I need variety."

So in addition to repeating the exercises Madame Beaufort and Kat taught in class, Jenny turned to the ballet books her father had taken out of the library for her. She flipped through their pages during lunch hours at school, looking for different enchainments— sequences of steps—to challenge Ara with. Not surprisingly, the exercises Ara liked best were the allegro. But Jenny knew the adagio were what Ara really needed to practise.

Naturally, Jenny stayed away from the harder movements that were intended for higher grades and dancers much older than they were, but that still gave her plenty of material to draw upon.

Meanwhile, as keen as Ara was to work on developing her new skills, she didn't neglect Jenny's needs.

"I had an idea about how to help you," Ara said one Friday, after they had finished their warm-up. "Remember that time in Kat's class when we did the mirror improvisation?"

Jenny remembered. Kat had divided the students into partners. One person in each pair was the leader and could dance whatever steps she liked. The other partner had to stand opposite the leader and copy her movements in sync, just like a mirror.

"I'm not sure I could do that," said Jenny. "You'd be watching me, and that makes me nervous."

Ara raised one eyebrow mischievously. "What if we turned the lights off first? Then I couldn't see you."

"But if it's dark, how could I see to follow you?"

"Ha ha ha!" said Ara, laughing villainously. "That's where my cunning plan comes in." She went over to the games shelf and pulled out what looked like a large pile of greenish-yellow bangles and rings. "See these? Glow in the dark! They're left over from Halloween. My dad was giving one away with every video rental." Ara put bangles on her wrists, forearms, and ankles. She slid glow-in-the-dark rings on her fingers and tied them to the strings of her ballet slippers. She looped flexible glow-in-the-dark strips around the tops of her calves. She clipped a few rings to a headband and put it on her head. Finally, she put a string through the remaining bits of jewelry and tied it around her waist.

"See," said Ara triumphantly. "Now with the lights off, you can see what I'm doing, but I won't be able to see you!"

Jenny blinked. "You come up with the craziest ideas."

"What can I say?" Ara replied. "I like props. So I'll be the leader, okay?"

Jenny couldn't find a reason to object, so she agreed. Ara turned the CD player on and the lights out. She walked back to Jenny and stood two feet in front of her. Ara's headband glowed like a tiara in the dark, and her body looked like it was shimmering with fairy dust.

When the music began, Ara began to improvise. She moved slowly at first. By following the little coloured lights that indicated where Ara's hands, feet, head, and waist were, Jenny had no trouble making her own body stay in sync. After a few minutes, Jenny started to relax. Another few minutes passed, and she realized she was having fun.

Then the music grew faster, and Ara's movements sped up as well. Jenny had to pay very close attention. Sometimes she couldn't respond quickly enough and had to skip a movement in order to catch up to Ara. But the great thing about having the lights off was that Ara couldn't know whether Jenny was making mistakes or not.

When Jenny realized she couldn't keep up any longer, she stopped, felt her way along the wall to the light switch, and flipped it on.

Ara stopped what she was doing and turned off the CD. "How did it go?"

"Pretty good," Jenny said, a little breathless.

"Come on back over here."

Jenny came back to the centre of the room.

"What do you think? Are you ready to try it with the lights on?"

Jenny took a deep breath. "Okay," she said nervously.

Ara started the CD from the beginning again, and Jenny began to mirror her once more. It actually was less scary now than she had expected. But all the same, she avoided looking directly into Ara's eyes.

Partway through the second song, Ara said, "Okay, now you lead."

Jenny froze. So did Ara. Jenny nervously took a step back and started to reach for a lock of hair to twist. So did Ara. Jenny laughed. Ara laughed too.

Well, if Ara was determined to imitate her, Jenny decided she may as well do something more interesting. So she started moving deliberately—first just her arms and head and then her feet, trying not to worry what Ara thought of her choices. Ara was very good at following.

"Want to try something harder?" Ara asked after the second song started.

"Sure," said Jenny.

"Get ready. Now let's both lead and follow at the same time."

This was harder. With no designated leader, they had to move in sync by guessing what each other wanted to do, by cooperating very closely and taking turns initiating movements. It was like trying to mind read. But strangely enough, after a few awkward moments at the beginning, they were able to do it.

By the time Ara's mother called them upstairs to dinner that night, Ara and Jenny both felt elated and exhausted. Reaching the top of the basement stairs, they found Mrs. Reyes waiting for them. "I just wanted to say, I can tell how hard you girls are working, and I am very proud of both of you for taking the time to help each other," she said. "You know, whenever you work at something, you get results. And when you can help each other as friends, the results will be even better. So I am looking forward to seeing you both dance very beautifully in this year's ballet." She turned to Jenny. "I phoned your mother to let her know how hard you are working because I thought she should know, so she can be proud too."

Jenny wasn't sure how her mother would have taken this news, and she didn't dare say there was no way she could find the courage to dance in front of an audience. But she felt grateful to Mrs. Reyes for doing her such a favour, so she just stammered, "Thanks."

Mrs. Reyes walked back toward the kitchen, where dinner was waiting to be brought to the table. Ara whispered to Jenny, "This is great. Now I can ask her for pointe shoes and she'll have to say yes!"

Chapter 16

Secret Spilled

For a brief moment on her way home that day, Jenny wondered if her mother would take Mrs. Reyes's phone call as the "sign" that volunteering at ballet was worthwhile. It turned out she did not. "It's not enough to work hard," her mother explained at the dinner table that evening. "I want to see some real results."

Jenny's father, on the other hand, seemed more impressed by the effort Jenny was making. When Jenny started to sort laundry after breakfast the next morning, one of her regular Saturday chores, her father surprised her by saying, "I'll do that. You go get ready for your volunteer work."

Ara arrived for dance class that day during the forty-five minute break after Veronique's private lesson and before Grade Four Ballet. This was the time when Jenny usually ate lunch in the waiting room. Sometimes Kat joined her, but today she had some work to do in the office, so Jenny was by herself when Ara bounced in.

"Hi. You're here early," Jenny said, setting down her sandwich.

"I had an idea," Ara announced, as she flopped down on the couch beside Jenny. "No one's here yet, are they?"

"Just us," said Jenny.

"Why don't we go into the studio and do a little practice before class? You've never danced on a sprung floor before, have you?"

Jenny hesitated. "I do a little bit when I'm helping out in the morning classes." Jenny decided not to mention that Kat had taken a few minutes that morning to give her some corrections. She didn't want Ara to feel left out.

"I know—a few stretches and *demi-pliés*. But what about some of the things I've seen you do at my place? It's way more fun when you have a big space to move in. Besides, the more you become used to dancing in the studio, the braver you'll be about participating in a real class."

Jenny thought about this. There had been times when Jenny found the studio empty—either before or after class—that she had been tempted to try out the real barre or see how far she could leap when there was no chance of bumping into furniture. But her fear that someone might burst in unexpectedly had always stopped her. "Okay," she said hesitantly, "as long as we stop before anyone else arrives."

"Great," said Ara. "Meet me in the studio in five minutes."

Jenny quickly finished her lunch while Ara ran off to the girls' change room to get into her leotard, tights, and slippers. When they met in the studio a few minutes later, Kat was still busy elsewhere. The room was empty.

"Let's close the door, okay?" Jenny asked. "In case anyone else arrives early."

"Okay," said Ara. She pushed the door most of the way shut.

"Let's start with the barre," Ara suggested.

Jenny stepped up to the barre and put one hand on its polished wooden surface. She put her feet and other arm in first position. Ara came over and leaned against the barre, facing Jenny. "Go on," said Ara, "try a *grande plié!*"

Jenny raised her heels and bent her knees until she was as low to the ground as she could go, executing what she hoped was a graceful *port de bras* at the same time. Then she straightened, just as gracefully and controlled as before.

Next, Jenny and Ara ran through some of the enchainments the class had done the previous Thursday. Jenny found that the big space did feel liberating. The sprung floor felt gentler on her feet as well.

"Now how about an arabesque? Bet you never saw yourself do one in a mirror this big before." Jenny complied, glancing in the mirror as she held the position. Maybe it did look all right. Well, perhaps with some fine tuning.

Jenny pulled her eyes away from the mirror to look at Ara, who had a strangely broad smile on her face. "What?" Jenny asked. "I know, it needs work."

"No, that was perfect. It's just that ... I have a surprise for you," Ara announced.

"Look over there." Ara waved in the direction of the doorway. "See," she called out. "I told you she could do it!"

Jenny turned around to follow Ara's gaze. The door swung open, and Trish, Kristen, and Lian ran into the studio. They had obviously been watching Jenny through the crack in the door for some time. Jenny gasped and covered her mouth with her hands. The room started to sway. Her stomach somersaulted.

The other girls crowded around Jenny. They were speaking, but to Jenny their words were just a jumble of noise. Jenny turned to Ara, eyes wide open, seeking help.

Ara looked surprised and concerned as she put a reassuring hand on Jenny's shoulder. "It's okay," she said. "I just thought it was about time someone else saw how well you can dance."

Jenny's legs started to buckle. "I need some air," she said, and she ran out of the studio. Once again, the fire exit seemed her only escape. She pushed the crash bar, and the door swung open. For a moment, the fire alarm seemed to amplify the ringing in her hears. Then she slammed the door shut behind her, and it went silent.

Jenny held tightly onto the railing, deeply breathing in the cool air blowing in from the lake, trying to calm herself. A few seconds later, she heard the door open and the alarm go off again. She turned and saw that Ara had followed her out.

Jenny glared at Ara as she pressed her back against the corner of the railing. She didn't want to be with Ara just now. But Ara showed no sign of leaving. She just stood and looked at Jenny, smiling apologetically.

Jenny turned and focused on the lake. After a few breaths, she spun back, looked Ara right in the eye and said, "Don't ever, ever do that again!"

Ara looked shattered. "What's wrong?"

"You arranged for them to be there," Jenny spat accusingly.

"Yes," said Ara.

"Why? So they could laugh at me?"

"No." Ara looked genuinely distressed. "I thought it would help you to hear someone else tell you how good you are. You know, so you could feel more confident. So I phoned some people this morning and told them you were really this amazing dancer, but you were just a little shy ..."

"I didn't want anyone to see me. Not yet." Jenny was breathing rapidly. She could feel tears starting to form in the corners of her eyes. She brushed them away. "It was just our secret until I was ready. Now I can never go back in there."

"I'm sorry," Ara said. "I was sure you'd feel braver once you saw everyone's reaction."

"It's too soon. I'm not ready."

Ara put her hands on Jenny's shoulders and looked into her eyes. "Did you hear anyone laughing at you? Or making fun of you?"

Jenny looked up at the sky and then down at her toes. "I didn't actually hear what they said."

"You want to be part of the dance class, don't you?"

"Eventually."

"Come on back, please," said Ara. "You can just sit and watch like usual. Everyone wants you to."

Jenny tried to calm her breathing and focus her thoughts. Finally, she said, "I'll come on one condition: that you promise you'll never do this again. Promise me, no more surprises."

"Okay," said Ara. "I promise. I'm sorry."

Jenny wiped her eyes again. For a moment, she thought the impulse to run and hide would reassert itself. But instead, she took a deep breath and a small step forward.

Ara turned, stretched her hand toward the door, and stopped. For the first time, and at the same time, both of them noticed that there was no handle on the outside of the door. They looked at each other and started to laugh. Then they began the long walk down the fire escape stairs and around to the front door.

Back in the studio, Jenny and Ara found Lian, Trish, and Kristen waiting for them.

"You guys almost got us in trouble," Trish complained. "Madame Beaufort came in and asked who kept setting off the fire alarm."

"Never mind that," said Lian. "Why didn't you tell us you could dance, Jenny? That was great."

Jenny could feel her face burning. "I was just messing around before," she said. "I can't really dance."

"Looked pretty good for someone who's only ever sat against the wall," said Kristen. "You should join the class today."

All three girls plied Jenny with questions. They seemed impressed that she could have learned so much on her own. When Madame Beaufort arrived and began the class, Jenny still felt light-headed but also happier. It was as though she was really a part of the group for the first time. And that was a strange and wonderful feeling.

Jenny forgave Ara by the end of the class. Sitting against the wall, she realized that Ara had just been acting true to form and that she couldn't have imagined the effect her surprise would have on Jenny. Ara had done what she did out of friendship. And if one crisis was the price of having a friend who cared enough to want to help, then Jenny was willing to pay it ... provided, of course, that Ara kept her promise. No way did Jenny want anyone else watching her dance again, not until she was sure she was good enough.

After class, Ara and Jenny were the last to leave the change room.

"Oh," Ara said. "I almost forgot. There's something I want to show you." She grabbed her dance bag and slid along the bench to be closer to Jenny. Reaching into the bag, she pulled out something pink and satiny.

Jenny looked closely. It was a pair of pointe shoes.

"Cool, eh?" said Ara. "My mom bought two pairs for me. The fitting took forever, but they feel great."

"You've tried them on?" Jenny asked, a little concerned.

"Just in the store. Don't worry, I haven't tried dancing en pointe yet. I thought we could start on Tuesday. It's killing me to wait, but like you said, I want to do it right."

Chapter 17

Breakthroughs

On Sunday afternoon, Jenny closed herself in her room so she could review her notes on Veronique's private lessons. Fortunately, Kat had let her sit in on most of them. She had carefully written down all the exercises Kat was having Veronique practise in order to develop the ability to dance en pointe. She hoped Ara wouldn't be disappointed. Most of the work seemed dull and repetitious.

Next, Jenny rifled through her collection of ballet books, looking for more information on pointe work. There wasn't much detail, apart from repeated warnings against going en pointe at too young an age. It seemed like the authors of these books were more interested in discouraging girls from risking injury than explaining how to develop the skill. That was a scary thought. Nonetheless, the books did say that quite a few girls as young as twelve had learned to dance en pointe, at least the basic steps.

On Tuesday, after Jenny and Ara finished their usual practice, Ara announced, "I can't wait any longer!" She brought out her new pointe shoes. "The lady at the store showed me how to sew on the ribbons," Ara explained as she slipped the shoes on and tied the ribbons around her ankles. "She used to dance herself."

That's a relief, thought Jenny. Kat must have shown Veronique how to attach and tie the ribbons on pointe shoes before Jenny started volunteering because Jenny had never seen it done.

"Okay," said Ara, once she had the shoes on properly. "Now what?"

Jenny sat on the floor next to Ara and fished in her dance bag for her notebook. "Well, the one thing all the books say is that you have to go slowly. Build up your strength and balance gradually over months. You start with exercises facing the barre and then move on to parallel later on. You shouldn't try to balance on one foot until you're comfortable with two-footed positions. And it can take a long time before you're ready to move away from the barre."

Ara frowned. "Sounds a bit boring. Can't we just skip some of that?"

Jenny looked up from her notes. "Veronique's only doing two feet. And Kat won't let her move away from the barre yet, except for just walking."

"Yeah," Ara protested. "But I only have a couple of months, and I need to get better than Veronique, not just as good as."

Jenny pulled out another book from her bag and opened it to a page with illustrations. "I've been doing some reading. See here? This shows the position your feet have to be in when you're en pointe. You have to get in the habit of doing it perfectly each time."

Ara looked closely at the page while Jenny explained, "If you roll your feet too far forward, or not forward enough, or if you don't have the right alignment, you can injure yourself so badly over time that you have to stop dancing altogether forever."

"I might have to stop dancing soon anyway," said Ara, "if my dad gets his way!"

"But what if he doesn't?" said Jenny. "What if you get a solo part this year, and your dad lets you keep dancing, and one day you get a chance to become a famous ballerina—except by then your feet are so damaged you have to quit? And no one ever gets to see how great you could have been."

Jenny paused and looked Ara in the eye, making sure this last point sunk in. "Okay, I get it," Ara said. "But you'll watch me, right? And let me know if I'm doing it wrong?"

"I'll do my best. But you know I'm no expert."

"I know. But I have to try, and you're all I've got. Besides, you're better than you give yourself credit for."

"Okay. But please, just go slow at first."

"I will," Ara consented.

"I have something else too," said Jenny. She reached into her dance bag again and pulled out her DVD player. "I videoed Veronique's last private lesson, when she wasn't watching. Well, the part where she was practising pointe work anyway. It's just a few minutes long. But I thought we could play it so you could see what it looks like when she does it right."

"Excellent!" said Ara.

They played the video, pausing it to look at Veronique's alignment whenever Kat praised her. Then it was Ara's turn.

"For the first time," Jenny explained, "you should probably start with just some *relevés*. That's what Kat had Veronique do. Some in first position, some in fifth—with straight legs in the beginning."

"Okay," said Ara. She jumped up, walked over to the shelf they were using as a barre, and stood facing it in first position. "Now what?"

Jenny stood beside her, reading from her notes. "You have to be fully turned out, with your leg and stomach muscles pulled up as tight as you can. Eyes facing forward. Don't look at your feet. You can use the shelf for balance, but don't put any weight on it. Your legs and feet have to do the work, not the shoe, and not your arms.

"Gotcha," said Ara.

"Now, starting with straight legs, you're going to slowly roll up to *demi-pointe* and then give an extra push with your toes to take you into full pointe."

"Anything else?" Ara asked.

"Coming down is supposed to be the hardest part. You have to maintain control, keep your muscles pulled up, and roll your foot down—just the reverse of going up. If you think you can't hold it, let me know and I'll grab you."

It was probably fortunate that Ara had been practising so intensely over the past few weeks. Her feet and legs had become stronger than ever. Even so, this was the first time Jenny had seen Ara look nervous about anything. Or was she just excited? With Ara, it was hard to tell.

Ara took a deep breath. She began with a *relevé* to *demi-pointe*— slowing rising onto the balls of her feel in a controlled manner and then just as slowly down. Then she did the movement again. "Okay, here goes." Rising to *demi-pointe* a third time, she paused and then made a small spring onto the tips of her toes, held it for a moment, and then reversed down again. "Ahhh!" she yelled.

"What's the matter?" Jenny asked, grabbing Ara around the waist to support her. "Did you hurt yourself?"

"No," said Ara. "It's just that … I was en pointe!" Her face was ecstatic. "I'm going to do it again!"

Jenny stepped back to watch as Ara repeated the movement a few more times, never remaining on her toes for more than a second or two. During Ara's third try, Jenny squatted beside her to check her alignment. "A little farther forward," she said. "Pull everything up." Ara adjusted so that her big toe and ankle were in a straight line with her leg. "That looks better," said Jenny.

"It feels better too," said Ara, as she lowered her heels back to the floor.

"Want to try it in fifth?"

"Yes!"

Ara was a fast learner and got the hang of *relevés* in fifth position en pointe perfectly after just two tries. So Jenny suggested she attempt one more exercise. "The other thing Kat had Veronique do early on was to start with a *demi-plié* and then spring up onto pointe in one move. Just a couple of repetitions. And remember to roll down, just like you've been doing."

Altogether, Ara's first bit of pointe work lasted less than ten minutes. She would have kept going, but Jenny's conscience made her insist that Ara stop after that.

"Wah-hoo!" Ara yelled as she let go of the shelf and pranced across the room. And then, without thinking, she suddenly sprung onto one foot, en pointe. She came down just as quickly, wincing with pain. "Okay, bad idea. Bad idea."

Ara hobbled over to a chair.

"Are you all right?" Jenny asked, rushing over.

"I think so." Ara untied her pointe shoe, slid it off, and felt her toes. "I'm okay. But I think I will stick to two feet for a while."

Jenny made Ara promise she wouldn't do any pointe work without her or a teacher watching. Nonetheless, she felt proud of Ara for being brave enough to try the most difficult part of ballet.

Over the next few weeks, leading up to the Christmas break, Ara devoted five to ten minutes out of each of her sessions with Jenny to pointe work. At first, she stuck with *relevés*, in first, fifth, and sometimes second position, as well as simple walking exercises to get used to the shoes. After a while, she added *plies en pointe*, *sous-sus*, and *échappés*—steps in which her toes had to change position as she sprang onto them. Her balance improved, and so did the amount of time she was able to stay on her toes. After that first impulsive try, Ara agreed not to try *piqués*, or any other step that required balancing on one foot, until she was completely comfortable on two feet. But seeing her progress, Jenny knew it wouldn't take her long.

Meanwhile, Ara kept encouraging Jenny to do more improvisation with her. "To improvise, you have to not care what anyone around you thinks," Ara argued. "And if you can do that, then dancing choreographed steps will be easy."

With that in mind, Ara insisted they play a CD during each practice and improvise dancing to it. Some days Ara would sneak into Nadda's room and borrow one of her CDs (she always had a pile of them on her dresser). But after Nadda complained loudly one day, Jenny began bringing CDs with her, usually chosen at random from her parents' collection.

Jenny found slow songs to be the easiest to improvise to at first, but as she became more relaxed, she began to find fast songs enjoyable too. Ara had a lot more stamina than Jenny and could easily improvise for an entire CD without a break. Often, Jenny would stop after the first few songs and sit down to watch Ara. Jenny especially enjoyed it when Ara did some step or gesture that made Jenny think of an image or part of a story.

One morning, as Jenny was getting ready to leave for school, she remembered that she hadn't chosen a CD for her after-school practice with Ara. Not having much time, she ran to the CD rack in her father's office and grabbed a CD without looking at the case.

When she pulled the CD out of her bag at Ara's later that day, Jenny noticed that the disc she had picked was unlabelled. "I don't know what this CD is," she explained. "I just found it on the shelf."

Ara shrugged. "Mystery music, eh? Well, let's see what it sounds like."

Ara slid it into the CD player, and a piano solo began playing through the speakers. "Sounds all right," she said. "Let's try it."

Jenny moved into the middle of the floor, putting a little space between her and Ara, who immediately plunged into a series of big leaps and turns. As usual, Jenny started small, gently swaying to the music, not quite comfortable enough yet to let herself go.

The floor was never quite big enough for Ara, and soon she was literally dancing circles around Jenny to avoid hitting walls. It occurred to Jenny that Ara was like a bird—a sparrow, or perhaps a swallow, darting through the air in search of insects. Whereas Jenny felt more like a flower rooted in the earth. She stretched her arms up, and they felt like petals reaching toward the light.

As the music continued, Jenny felt more and more that her feet were rooted to the ground, immovable. Only, she didn't want to be rooted. Her arms reached to all directions in turn, and she realized she wanted to fly, to pull herself into the air. Yet her feet wouldn't move. Ara, meanwhile, was becoming more birdlike in her movements. She swooped and soared around the room, driven by the sheer joy of flight.

"Where do you want to go?" Jenny called out.

"To the moon!" Ara responded, sensing this was part of the improvisation.

"Then take me with you," Jenny called.

"I can't. I'm being buffeted." Ara mimed being blown about by random bursts of wind.

"Take me with you!"

At that point, the first track on the CD ended and a new one with a faster pace began. Ara danced over to Jenny, grabbed her waist, and spun her around. "Don't let go," Ara instructed.

Jenny struggled to keep her feet moving in sync with Ara as Ara pulled and pushed her around the room in time to the music. It was like Ara was taking her on a journey to places she couldn't go on her own. Back and forth they went across the floor. Ara was making Jenny do steps she had been too nervous to try on her own and steps she had never seen before. As the third track began, Ara let go and soared off on her own while Jenny came to a stop and sat down near the shelf.

This new piece was faster still. To Jenny it suggested a battle, or perhaps an ocean with waves whipped high by ferocious winds. Ara was like a little soldier dodging enemies.

Jenny grabbed her notebook. She took out the pen she kept inside the spiral binding and began to write. By the time the music ended, Jenny was scribbling furiously. Ara, finally winded, came over to ask what she was doing.

"I had an idea," Jenny said excitedly. "For a ballet."

"Really?"

"Yes. It's all about a flower that wants to fly and a swallow that wants to visit the moon. So the swallow agrees to pluck the flower and take her with her so they could both see. And they have to fight winds and pirates at sea and visit the moon people, and when they have seen it all, the flower bursts into those seed-parachute things that carry the swallow safely back to earth and when the seeds sprout the new flowers look like little moons." Jenny paused her writing for a second and looked at Ara. "I know it sounds a bit stupid."

"It's not," said Ara. "It's a great idea."

"Thanks. There's more to the story. I started to see it all when we were improvising."

"You should write it all down. Then, next time we practise, we can try dancing it."

"Okay," said Jenny.

"Just one thing," Ara said, "when we do it on stage, I want to be the swallow."

Chapter 18

A Real Ballet

That evening, just before she turned out her light to sleep, Jenny put the mystery CD into her player. Then she lay in bed with the headphones on and closed her eyes, listening to the music. As her body slowly relaxed, she watched the story unfold in her mind.

At five thirty the next morning, Jenny woke up with her ears sore from the pressure of the headphones. The CD was still playing. She must have accidentally set the player on repeat. But the entire ballet, from beginning to end, was now as clear as if it were a film. She had seen it in her dreams.

Jenny took off the headphones and turned off the CD player. She got up, switched on her desk light, and found her notebook and a pencil. She had a fear she might forget everything if she didn't record it quickly. In fact, parts were already starting to fade.

Jenny opened her notebook and began drawing furiously. By six o'clock, she had filled ten pages with sketches.

As the Christmas holidays approached and a thick layer of snow built up over every lawn, the idea of creating her ballet refused to leave Jenny's mind. In no way did she feel up to the task of translating her rough drawings into actual dance steps. Yet the idea had caught hold of her and was not about to let go.

Meanwhile, Ara and Jenny continued to meet three times a week. Their work together was becoming nearly as structured as the ballet classes at the school. First, they would spend forty-five minutes practising everything Kat and Madame taught. Then Ara would do her pointe work exercises, with Jenny's help, for ten minutes or so. Finally, they would spend half an hour on improvisation, which was intended to help Jenny.

Jenny insisted that their improvisations now had to revolve around her ideas for the ballet. She wanted to see if what she had imagined could really work as a dance. This suited Ara just fine.

Before each improvisation, Jenny would show Ara one of her sketches and then explain her ideas for that part of the story. Then they would play the CD track that went with that part and improvise dancing to it. Scenes that needed more than two dancers were tricky, but the girls took the various roles in turn and repeated the improvisation several times.

During the day at school, Jenny often found herself thinking about her ballet when she was supposed to be doing seat work. Then she would remember her promise to her mother not to fall behind in school and would hurry to complete her work in time.

Of course, recesses and lunch hour were a different matter. Then Jenny was free to find a quiet corner of the school yard, take out her pencil and sketchbook, and play with ideas for the ballet on paper or else try to sketch what she and Ara had improvised the day before. The more she thought, the more ideas about how to improve the dance or fill in missing parts popped into her head. Soon she was spending most of her free time at school filling up pages of her sketchbook.

Jenny very much wanted the ballet to be both her and Ara's creation. She valued the fact that Ara had more experience dancing. Ara could often look at a sketch and tell right away whether the steps Jenny drew could actually be danced. But, unlike Jenny, Ara didn't tend to have ideas she could put into words, nor did she think about the ballet between practices. Her creativity emerged while she was on her feet improvising. She could take one of Jenny's ideas and play with it—improvising any number of variations and extensions that brought it to life.

Usually they improvised together, but sometimes, Jenny just called out ideas while Ara took different characters in turn and improvised until the dance looked right. Watching Ara, Jenny could see immediately whether a particular step or combination looked good. And that was usually faster and better than when Jenny tried to plan steps in her head. Seeing what worked or didn't work in improvisation gave Jenny new ideas about how to improve or add to the steps they had worked on before and what steps to delete. Gradually, as they worked in this way, the story became more defined and detailed, the choreography more fixed.

On Christmas morning, Jenny found in her stocking a set of tickets to *The Nutcracker*. The National Ballet's touring company was performing it for one night only at the Grand Theatre the day after Boxing Day. "This is great! Thank you," Jenny said to her parents. "But why are there four tickets?"

"I thought you might like to ask Ara to join us," her father explained.

"I would," said Jenny, and she phoned Ara that day to invite her.

It was the first time in her life that Jenny had seen live ballet. But from the moment the lights went down, she was mesmerized. The music was performed by a live, full-piece orchestra. The lighting effects were magical. The costumes and sets were richly detailed. And best of all, the dancers were superb. Their strength and grace rendered Jenny breathless. She wished she had been allowed to bring her camcorder.

At intermission and on the car ride home, Jenny talked excitedly with Ara about how some of the staging for *The Nutcracker* could be adapted for their ballet, which they had decided to call *The Moonflower and the Swallow*. Ara was particularly taken with the ballerina who played the Sugar Plum Fairy. "I wish some day I could dance like her," she said.

The spring term at the Kingston Ballet School was scheduled to start midway through January. Ara was still very determined to challenge Veronique's place as the lead dancer for the school's year-end recital. Although neither of the teachers had mentioned the recital since the open house, Ara knew they would soon start rehearsing parts of it in class. She wanted her dancing skills to be at their peak, and to be noticed, before any casting decisions were made, so she worked harder than ever when she and Jenny got together. She found she had to wrap her toes in cotton each day to cut down on blisters.

At their last practice before the start of the term, Jenny asked if they could run through a section of *The Moonflower and the Swallow* they had yet to work on. "We've got the start of the story pretty much set. If we get the Sparrow's return down, it will feel like the whole thing is coming together."

"I don't mind," Ara agreed, "as long as we do our warm-ups first."

The girls did a quick warm-up, and then Jenny described her idea for the scene. "Do you have a couple of old umbrellas?" she asked Ara.

"I think so. Why?"

"I thought we could use those for the parachute seeds. You could have one in each hand as you're coming down to earth."

"Cool," said Ara. She ran upstairs to search for umbrellas while Jenny put the mystery CD in the player.

Ara returned a few minutes later with two plastic umbrellas. "Nadda and I used these when we were little. They're the smallest ones we have."

"Great," said Jenny. "I thought of something else too. Would you mind if we videoed our improv? I brought my camcorder."

"I don't mind. I'd like to see how it looks since I can never watch myself dancing. What made you think of it?"

"I just thought I could use it in case I forget anything."

Jenny took the camcorder out of her bag, put in a fresh disc, and set it up on a table, where its lens could take in most of the room. "Now, we just have to remember that the camera is the audience."

Ara programmed the CD player to play the track they needed. Then she pressed the play button. When the first note sounded, Ara began to improvise. Jenny wanted this part to be spectacular since it was very close to the end of the ballet. Even though Ara's first try was pretty good, Jenny insisted they go over the section many times, trying different movements and making improvements. When they played back the video on the camcorder's tiny screen, Ara said, "It looks great. Just like a real ballet."

Though she wouldn't admit it, Jenny too felt happy with what they had created.

"Can I borrow the DVD?" Ara asked when Jenny was packing her dance bag to go home. "I'll give it back to you after class on either Saturday or Monday."

Jenny said, "Sure," and handed over the disc. "I won't have time to look at it before then anyway."

Chapter 19

Artists and Imposters

The next day, Saturday, was the first ballet class of the new term. Ara was ready. She danced with a technique so impeccable that even Madame Beaufort had to acknowledge her progress. Veronique's dancing had undeniably improved over the past four months too, but she looked quite put out to see how well Ara was doing.

However, it was Kat's Monday class on which everything hinged. Madame Beaufort had let everyone know that Kat would be evaluating the students that day and that those evaluations would have a big influence on what role everyone would dance in the year-end recital.

Ara arrived early for ballet class on Monday. She had put her hair into a bun rather than her usual pigtails. In the change room, she pulled on a brand new pair of tights. Jenny had never seen Ara wear tights that didn't have at least one hole in them, and she guessed that Ara—for the second time ever—was nervous.

"Remember," Jenny whispered to her, "just keep it simple. No extra flourishes. Just show Kat what you can do."

Because Kat had not yet introduced pointe work to the class,

Ara could not show off her growing skill in that area without getting into trouble. Veronique, on the other hand, thanks to her private lessons with Kat, felt she had no such constraint. She made a big show of putting on her pointe shoes in the change room in front of everyone.

It was a great relief to Ara, and a crushing blow to Veronique, when Kat told Veronique not to go en pointe during class that day. "I need to see everyone doing the same steps," Kat explained. "But don't worry. We'll begin pointe work in class in the next few weeks."

Kat had a clipboard with her that day. During barre work, she walked down the line taking notes and paying close attention to what every student was doing.

Kat kept her clipboard on her knee as she sat on her stool during the adagio portion of class, letting Jenny work the CD player. The class did fewer exercises that day but repeated them more times. Kat seemed to want everyone to get multiple tries. Adagio was where Veronique and Lian had always excelled. But Jenny thought Ara's performance was easily on a par with theirs.

Next came the allegros. This was where Jenny expected Ara to shine, and she did. Her control and precision even in the liveliest steps made her exciting and beautiful to watch.

No one expected Kat to make time for improvisation that day. But she did. After asking Jenny to play a particular track on the CD player, she gave each student sixty seconds to improvise, by themselves, in the centre of the studio floor.

Veronique had obviously been practising this. She was a little less stiff than usual, and she seemed to be making some effort at making steps up as she went. But to Jenny, she still looked like she was trying to think her way through the exercise rather than follow her feelings.

Ara's turn was last. Everyone expected her to do something crazy and off the wall, as usual. Instead, Ara began small, dipping her head to one side and moving one foot along the floor in a lazy *ronde de jambe*. The music Kat had chosen felt slow, sad, and lonely, and Ara's movements reflected that feeling perfectly.

Then the music's tempo began to pick up, and Ara's movements intensified. Her arms and face conveyed the emotional transition beautifully. Jenny could feel tears building in her eyes. As the music grew bigger, Ara's movements grew bigger. She crossed the space back and forth using mostly steps drawn from classical ballet but at the same time adding her own inventions. She pirouetted, leaped, and then surprised everyone by incorporating floor work. Sixty seconds passed, and no one seemed to notice. Everyone in the room was entranced. Finally, when the music ended, most of the class burst into applause—except of course for Veronique, who looked like she was choking on her disappointment.

When Jenny went to the girls' change room after class, some of the girls were congratulating Ara on her improvisation. "I can't believe you didn't rehearse that," Trish said.

"Well, to be honest, Jenny and I have been practising a lot outside class," Ara explained, looking at Jenny.

"Jenny and you?" Veronique asked, sounding surprised.

"Yeah, she's really helped me a lot. She's even come up with an idea for a ballet."

"No way!" said Robyn, taken aback.

"Way!" said Ara.

"You would take help from someone who can't dance?" Veronique scoffed. "What's that, the blind leading the blind? Or maybe it's 'birds of a feather flock together.'"

"Jenny can dance," said Trish.

"What's that supposed to mean?" Ara said to Veronique.

"It means I'll believe she can dance when I see it, which won't be anytime soon. And the same goes for you. I don't know what you call those steps you were doing, but they weren't ballet."

"Guys," Kristen interjected, "maybe you should take it down a notch, before you say something you'll regret."

But her words were a little late to have any effect on Ara. Her eyes were flashing anger as she stood on her feet and began to shout.

"You think you're such a prima ballerina! Jenny knows more about ballet than you ever will. And she's a better dancer. She just doesn't want to show it because she's afraid you'll throw a big hissy fit!"

"Yeah, right." Veronique slung her dance bag on her shoulder and headed for the door. Over her shoulder, she called back, "Did I mention I'm going to the National Ballet School next year? If you like, I'll send you a postcard."

Robyn stood up to follow her stepsister. "She hasn't even been accepted yet," she told the room and then walked out.

Ara turned to Jenny. "Don't listen to what she says. We know you can dance."

But Jenny didn't say a word in reply. She just shrugged her shoulders, threw her street clothes on overtop of her leotard, and ran out the door. When she climbed into the backseat of the family car, she had tears running down her sweatshirt that she couldn't possibly hide.

"What's wrong?" her father asked. He was driving Jenny home that day. "Did something happen?"

"Just drive, Dad, please," Jenny said, sniffling.

Her father put the car in gear and drove out of the parking lot. "Do you want to go straight home?" he asked.

"Doesn't matter."

Two blocks away, there was a small park on the shore of Lake Ontario. Her father parked the car at the edge of the park, facing the water, a Martello tower, and a large sculpture. There was hardly anyone there, so they could talk privately. He got out of the front seat and climbed in the back next to Jenny. "Tell me what happened," he said.

Jenny didn't know how to express what was going on emotionally inside her. She shrugged and wiped some of the tears off her face.

"Did something upsetting happen at the school today?"

Jenny turned and looked out the window. "Kat was evaluating everyone. Ara did well."

"Are you happy for her?"

Jenny nodded. "Yes. It was her best work ever."

"Then I guess you're not crying because of that."

Jenny took a breath and decided to try to explain. "It's just that ... I want to dance so much ... and I thought I was getting somewhere. I've learned so much. And when Ara and I are just us, I can do most things. I have this idea for a ballet ... that is, Ara and I have been working on it ... but the idea was mine at first ... The thing is, I like volunteering, and I like most people at the school ... but I don't know if I will ever be able to do it. I keep telling myself it will get better, that I'll learn to stop being afraid, but I don't know if I will."

Her father put his arm around her. "It sounds like you've come a long way. Why not give yourself a little more time?"

"I don't know. Maybe I should quit. I mean … maybe I'm just fooling myself."

Her father stroked her back. "I don't know what to tell you, sweetie, except that every artist feels that way at some point in their life. It's not easy to know the right choice. Sometimes the easier path may be best. But I also know that the only ones who make it are the ones who learn to keep going despite those feelings."

"But how do I know whether I'll be able to do it or not?"

Her father thought for a moment. "Did one of the teachers say you should quit?"

"No. But they've also never seen me dance."

"Maybe you should wait until they do. Maybe you should get the opinion of someone who knows what they're talking about before you give up. Besides, you're only twelve. The important thing for now is to just have fun."

Jenny didn't reply.

"Why don't you wait a little while? At least a few more weeks. See how things go. Maybe you can ask Katrina whether she thinks you have potential. If she does, you and I might be able to persuade Mom to let you take lessons again."

Jenny winced. "I don't know if it would make a difference. I still couldn't dance in class."

"Well, think about it. Things can change after all. Meanwhile, why don't we get something special to bring home for supper? Your choice."

A trace of a smile appeared briefly on Jenny's face. "Okay," she said. But inside, she felt her dream of becoming a dancer slowly evaporating.

Chapter 20

Secret Shattered

Kat had just eased herself into the chair in the school office to go over her notes when she heard a knock on the door.

"Come in."

It was Ara.

"Hello," said Kat. "Very nice work today, by the way. You've really made excellent progress this year."

"Thanks," said Ara.

"What can I do for you?"

"I want to talk to you about Jenny."

Kat sat back a little in her chair. "What about her?"

Ara stepped forward and leaned against the edge of the desk. "You may not know it, but she's a really good dancer."

"I know she's been doing some practising on her own."

"Well, not just on her own. With me too."

Kat gave her a stern look. "I hope you aren't trying to teach her yourself. A person needs a qualified teacher, especially when they're just starting out."

This wasn't what Ara wanted to talk about. "It's not that. Jenny would love to be taking classes. It's just that she has this phobia or something. It's holding her back."

"Yes, I've noticed."

"The thing is, she really is good. But hardly anyone knows. And I'm afraid she'll give up because she doesn't believe it either."

"That's something she may need to work out on her own."

"Yes, but … here's the thing. We've been working on this idea Jenny had for a ballet. It's really good. We even made a DVD of one of our rehearsals. If you could just watch it, you'll see what I mean." Ara rummaged in her dance bag for a moment, pulled out the DVD, and held it out.

"Does Jenny also want me to watch it?"

"Maybe not," Ara admitted. "But there's no other way you'll ever get to see it. I thought, if you think it's no good, then you don't ever have to tell anyone. But if you could see how talented she is … maybe it would just help if someone else knew."

Kat frowned. "I'd like to help. I'm not sure I should watch it without her permission."

"Please. It can just be our secret either way."

"You may have to tell her eventually. And she may not like you for it."

"That's okay. It's just that someone needs to see it, someone who knows ballet."

Kat thought for a moment. "I can see this is important to you. Can you leave it with me for a day or so? I can't promise you I'll look at it, but I'll consider it."

"Sure. Thanks. You won't be disappointed." Ara set the DVD on the desk and left.

By the time she went to bed on Monday, Jenny had made up her mind. She was quitting the dance school. Veronique was right. There was no way she'd ever have the courage to dance, so what was the point?

Ara was sure to get the lead role in the year-end show, after her brilliant performance on Monday, so she really didn't need Jenny's help anymore. Jenny phoned Ara and cancelled their Tuesday and Wednesday practices, making up a rather lame excuse that she had too much homework.

Jenny was a little bit nervous about telling Kat face-to-face that she would no longer be volunteering on Saturday mornings, but she couldn't just not show up either. So she decided to go to the Thursday Grade Four class, same as usual, and leave a resignation note for Kat in the office.

Jenny had her mother's permission to take the bus to the dance school after school. This meant that she arrived well before class. Only Robyn and Veronique ever came so early. Jenny did not want to face Veronique again. Fortunately, neither she nor her stepsister were in the waiting room when Jenny arrived.

The office door was slightly ajar. Jenny was about to knock when she heard Kat's voice from inside.

"You've been wanting to improve the standards in the school," Kat was saying. "This could be a unique opportunity."

"I wanted to raise the quality of the training," came Madame Beaufort's voice, "so students who were considering a career in dance would have a better chance of succeeding. I do not want to indulge in frivolous experiments. Nor do I think we should be turning our recitals into something akin to a Grade Five school assembly."

"But look at what these girls have done!" Kat insisted.

"Considering their age, it's remarkable. And you can't deny the improvement in Ara's case."

They must be discussing the casting for the recital, Jenny thought. *I hope Ara gets a solo role.*

Madame Beaufort made a noise that sounded like a scoff. "You never know what you'll get from that girl. Yes, occasionally, she can be very good, but the next time she'll throw all her training out the window and do something totally unexpected and sometimes dangerous."

"Have you ever known any other students their age who could come up with a piece of choreography this sophisticated?"

"No, which is why I suspect they are simply copying something they saw on television. Besides, I thought you didn't like story ballets."

"I don't mind story ballets. I just don't believe all the great ballets have been done already. At any rate, what these girls have done is no copy."

"How can you be sure?"

"There's too much of them in it. And too little of what I'd expect from a trained choreographer. Look, here, at this part coming up."

There was a pause. Then Madame Beaufort spoke again. "You must have taught her that."

"I didn't. Now listen to how she gives directions here. This is coming from her."

Jenny peered through the crack in the door. Madame Beaufort and Kat were looking at something on the TV set. If she pushed the door slightly, Jenny would be able to see what it was...

Moments later, Jenny was running as fast as she could out of the building. At the bottom of the metal steps outside, she collided with Ara, who was just arriving for class.

Jenny took one look at Ara's smiling face and allowed all of her righteous anger to explode out of her. "You gave them our DVD! After you promised no surprises!"

Ara looked taken aback. "Them? I loaned it to Kat."

"No one was supposed to see it!"

"I know," Ara protested. "But I just had to let Kat see it. The look on your face when you left last time … I was afraid you were going to quit. I just thought …"

"No, you didn't," Jenny interrupted. "You never think. You just do things without thinking about other people's feelings. All you care about is yourself." Tears were now welling up in her eyes.

"Look, you can't just live your life under a rock!" Ara shot back. "You can't just hide and expect the world to take notice of you. If you don't let people see you, you'll end up never doing anything, never dancing, never having fun."

"I don't want to talk to you anymore!" Jenny turned and ran away from Ara, away from the school, away from the parking lot where students were being dropped off. She ran down the street until she ran out of breath and was forced to slow to a walk.

So this was finally the end. No more dance school. No more practising. No more Ara. Her mother was right after all.

Jenny tried to picture herself in a Pathfinders uniform: cargo pants, a sporty T-shirt, a sash over one shoulder with badges sewn on it. Somehow, it didn't look right. But then, maybe a dance leotard was never the right fit for her either.

It was a long walk to Jenny's house. But she thought she could probably make it home before her mother left to pick her up after dance class.

Jenny had only gone a few blocks when a rusty compact car pulled up to the side of the street ahead of her and Kat got out.

"Jenny," Kat said, quickly striding up to her, "are you all right? Ara told us you'd left on your own."

It figures, Jenny thought. Ara couldn't even keep quiet about that. "I want to go home," she said.

"I understand. But there's no need walk all that way on your own. We phoned your parents. They're on their way to the school to pick you up. Let me give you a ride back to the school."

Jenny didn't feel she had the strength to argue. She meekly climbed into the passenger seat of Kat's car to let herself be driven back to the school.

Glancing at Jenny as she drove, Kat spoke. "Ara said you were upset because she had lent me the DVD of you and her."

Jenny felt her stomach tighten. She did not want to talk about this. "It's nothing," Jenny said. "We were just fooling around."

"Listen, Jenny, I've spent nearly my whole life in dance. I started when I was younger than you, in a school very like this one. I spent six years in the National Ballet School. I've had five years of post-secondary training, three years of teacher training, and three years as a soloist with the National Ballet. And for most of those years, I taught classes on the side. I know the difference between kids who are just fooling around and those who have real talent. What you two have created on your own is remarkable."

"Madame Beaufort didn't think so."

"Madame Beaufort has never worked in a professional dance company or attended a professional school."

"Really?"

Kat inhaled audibly as she turned the car into the parking lot. "I probably shouldn't have said that."

She brought the car to a stop and turned to face Jenny. "Don't misunderstand me. Madame Beaufort is a good teacher. She started this school out of a love for ballet and because, at the time, there was no other place in town where kids could get dance training. She has taken teacher training courses and worked hard to set high standards for this school. It's just that her perspective is a little different than mine. She likes the style of ballet that was popular thirty years ago, when she was a girl. Whereas I'm more interested in what the best professional companies are doing today.

"Listen, I'm only telling you this because I don't want you to be discouraged by anything she has said. I have something even more important that I want to talk to you about. But first, I hope you won't be too upset about what Ara did. She lent me the DVD because she cares about you. She's a good friend. She was afraid you would give up on dance before we discovered your potential. Please tell me you haven't given up."

Jenny chose to evade the question. She felt betrayed by Ara and found it difficult to hear what Kat was telling her. "What do you mean by 'potential'?"

Now it was Kat's turn to be evasive. Instead of answering, she asked another question. "That ballet you were working on, on that DVD—that was something you came up with on your own?"

"Well, both of us really. I mean, I thought up the story. Ara and I came up with the steps mostly through improvisation—just what you taught in class."

"But how did you do it? Tell me more about the process."

Jenny found this question a little confusing. In her mind, there wasn't anything special about what Ara and she had done. "Well, basically I would come up with ideas—pictures in my mind of things I'd like to see in the story. I'd make sketches. Then Ara and I would improvise steps. Sometimes we'd do it together. Other times I would watch her and call out ideas on how to make the dance better. Ara would try them, and if we liked them we kept them in."

"That's what you were doing on the DVD, isn't it?"

"Yes."

"But there were some steps, techniques really, that were on the video that you haven't seen in class. Where did you learn about them?"

"Some we just made up. Others I got from books. I've been looking up stuff to help Ara. She really deserves to get a lead role in the performance this year."

"You're probably right, but first things first. Let's wait for your parents inside."

Chapter 21

Prodigy

Kat and Jenny got out of the car and went back inside the dance school. Jenny wondered what exactly was going on. Still, she was glad Kat agreed with her about Ara.

Kat escorted Jenny into the dance school office and asked her to wait there until her parents arrived. A glance at the clock told Jenny that the Grade Four class would end in another twenty minutes. Kat, however, was back in five minutes, accompanied by Ara. She asked Ara to sit down and wait too.

Jenny didn't want to be sharing a room with Ara just now. She avoided looking her former friend in the eye. Ara, however, refused to accept this treatment and tried to engage Jenny in conversation.

"I'm sorry I lent Kat the DVD," Ara began. "I didn't mean to hurt your feelings. I just think ... you've got more talent than you realize. You helped me so much. I don't know why you're so afraid to let anyone else see because you're as good as anyone. And it's not about being the best anyway. Don't quit, whatever you do."

Jenny sat silent for some time, looking at the wall. Finally, she spoke. "How do you know I was thinking of quitting?"

Ara shrugged. "Just a guess. I mean, it must be frustrating not participating in the classes. And then to have to put up with what Veronique said."

Jenny was quiet again for a moment. "I know you're right," she confessed. "I mean, not about the talent part. Although, sometimes, when I think about it, I think I couldn't be that bad. I mean, I can't be worse than Robyn. Can I?"

Ara smiled. "Not by a mile."

"But I just don't like being looked at. Not when I don't know what people are thinking about me. It ties me up in knots."

"What if people were only thinking good things about you?"

"I guess I just don't think that's possible."

Ara thought for a moment. "I don't know where you got that crazy idea. But if I were you, I'd just do what I wanted anyway. Even if people still thought badly of me afterward, at least I'd have had fun."

Jenny turned to Ara and gave her a small smile. "It doesn't feel that easy to me."

"Are we still friends?" Ara asked. "Please, let's still be friends. I'd miss you if we weren't. I'd miss our practices together."

After a slight hesitation, Jenny said, "Still friends." Somehow, she could never stay angry with Ara for long.

After a few minutes, it occurred to Jenny to ask a question. "Why did Kat ask you to wait here? Did something happen in class?"

"No. She just came into the studio and got me."

There were still ten minutes of class left, according to the clock, when Kat reentered the room. This time, she was accompanied by Jenny's parents and Mrs. Reyes.

"Please, everyone have a seat," Kat began. There were not quite enough chairs, but Jenny's father settled for leaning against a file cabinet.

Kat took the chair behind the desk. "I have something I want to talk to all of you about. First, I want to let you know how well your daughters have been doing these past four months. Ara has made tremendous strides in class. And Jenny has been a big help as a volunteer. I imagine you know how hard they have been working outside of class, helping each other learn about ballet."

"It has been taking up a lot of Jenny's time," Jenny's mother noted.

"Ballet does ask a lot of us," Kat agreed. "And I'm afraid I want to ask something more from all of you."

Kat paused and looked at Jenny. "May I have your permission to talk about the DVD? I promise that I have only good things to say about it."

"Okay," said Jenny, wondering what Kat could possibly be leading up to.

Kat turned back to the adults. "Have the girls told you about the ballet they've been working on?"

"Oh, yes," said Mrs. Reyes immediately.

"No," said Jenny's parents, surprised.

"That's what I thought," said Kat. She looked at the Sparks. "Then I have a wonderful surprise for you. Jenny and Ara have come up with an idea for an original ballet."

"It's mostly Jenny's idea," said Ara.

"I've looked at a DVD they made of one of their rehearsals. What they have accomplished so far is very good, much better than I would have expected to see from students their age." Kat paused. "No, that's not strong enough. As I said, Ara's skills as a dancer have improved tremendously this year. However, I understand from the girls that much of the credit for the choreography goes to Jenny. And if that is true, then I suspect this school has discovered its first real prodigy."

Jenny's mother looked stunned for a moment. Her father stood upright. Both of them looked at Jenny and then back at Kat, as if they were not sure they had heard her correctly. "A prodigy?" her mother asked.

"Yes," said Kat.

"But I don't understand. I thought Jenny refused to dance."

"I don't mean she's an exceptional dancer, yet," Kat clarified. "Although that may come in time, if she overcomes her shyness. It's her conceptual abilities, her talent for choreography, that I think is extraordinary."

"That's fantastic," said Jenny's father.

Kat nodded. "It's almost unprecedented. What's more, I have had a long conversation with Madame Beaufort, and I have persuaded her to let me present their work for our year-end recital; that is, if I can have all of your support. I would prefer it if you would register Jenny as a student again. Apart from the fact that the school depends on the income from registrations, it would help satisfy the demands of our insurance policy. But even if she stays a volunteer, I would really like her to do this."

"I knew it," said Mrs. Reyes, looking at both girls. "I knew all your hard work would pay off."

"What exactly are you asking Jenny to do?" asked her mother.

"What I would like is for Jenny to continue the work she has been doing but with the school as a whole. I would like to mentor her, help her develop her ideas, to choreograph the ballet."

"And what about Ara?" asked Mrs. Reyes.

"I would like her to continue helping Jenny develop the piece and to dance whatever role she and Jenny choose."

"A solo part?" Ara asked.

"Yes," said Kat. "I may have to go to bat for you on that issue, but I believe you can do it."

"Just how much work would be involved?" Jenny's mother asked.

"There would be some extra rehearsals, but perhaps Jenny and Ara would be willing to compensate by doing more of their work in the school rather than out. That way, I can coach them better." Kat turned to Jenny. "The only thing is, Jenny, even if you don't dance in the ballet yourself, would you be willing to work with the other students the way you have been working with Ara?"

Jenny could hardly believe what Kat was asking her to do. And even if she could, could she see herself giving ideas and suggestions to everyone in the class, even Veronique? Would she be brave enough, strong enough, to make it work? "I'm not sure I could do that," she said.

"Surely we can have some time to think it over," said Jenny's mother.

"Yes, of course. It's a big decision," said Kat. "But remember, Jenny, I will be there to give you every bit of help you need. If you'd prefer, you could just tell me your ideas and I could work with the students. I want you to be comfortable with the process."

Kat turned back to the parents. "I have to say, I think it would be a really good thing for the school as well. To stage an original work, one choreographed by a student, would be a great experience for everyone."

"Thank you," said Jenny's father, and he offered to shake Kat's hand. "We'll talk this over and get back to you soon as possible."

"I look forward to it," said Kat. Then everyone exchanged good-byes and filed out.

"Isn't this great!" Ara whispered to Jenny as they walked toward the front entrance, trailing behind the adults.

"I guess," said Jenny, her knees feeling suddenly weak.

"Call me tonight if you can."

"This was a big surprise," said Jenny's father, once the Sparks were in their car and on their way home.

"Yes," said her mother. Turning around, she added, "I hope you realize, Jenny, I'm very proud of you, even if you decide not to do it."

"Surely she wants to do it," said her father.

"It's a lot of responsibility at her age."

"Yes, but she will have help. I don't think Katrina would have offered her the chance if she didn't believe she could do it."

"Even still. It may be a lot harder than she realizes. She won't want to let all those students down."

"What do you think, Jenny?" her father asked.

"I don't know yet," Jenny said. All the way home, her mind raced with thoughts of what just happened. She couldn't quite remember if Kat had said she wanted to choreograph Jenny's ballet or if she wanted to help Jenny choreograph the ballet. There was a big difference. One way meant that Jenny would be turning over what she and Ara had done so far to Kat to finish. It would be exciting to see what Kat did with it but also hard to let it go. The other way meant that Jenny would be in charge. And even with Kat helping, that was a pretty scary idea.

At least, either way, Ara would be able to dance a big role. But then Jenny remembered Veronique. How would she feel about getting replaced by Ara? Jenny could see her being pretty vindictive. And what would the others think about putting on Jenny's ballet, considering that Jenny had never even taken a dance class? How would they feel about Jenny being in charge? They'd probably resent it.

And then, would she actually want all that attention? Wouldn't it be easier to just keep doing what she was doing—just watch the rehearsals and the year-end recital from the sidelines? She'd never been involved in putting on a ballet before. Maybe it would be better to see how it was done first and get more involved in the next production, maybe after she found the courage to actually take lessons—if that day ever came.

That night, Jenny hardly slept at all. The decision that faced her was all too worrisome.

Chapter 22

A Tough Decision

By Saturday morning, Jenny had still not decided whether to accept Kat's offer. Her parents had debated the matter at every family meal since Thursday, with her father generally being in favour of Jenny's accepting it and her mother taking the opposite point of view. In the end, they decided to go along with whatever Jenny chose—register and pay for another term of lessons if she wanted to choreograph the ballet or let her continue as just a volunteer if she didn't.

Jenny mostly felt scared to death at the thought of taking on such a big role. What did she know about putting on a ballet? Yet beneath her fear, there was also excitement at the idea of seeing her ideas brought to life on stage. Sometimes she found herself trying to imagine which students at the school could dance certain roles the best. But then, it was also easy to imagine them not wanting to do a ballet she created.

In the end, Jenny went to the dance school for her regular Saturday morning volunteer work feeling 75 percent inclined to turn down the offer.

When Jenny entered the building, Robyn was standing in the

main corridor with her legs wide, doing some slow arm movements that looked nothing like ballet *port de bras*. Madame Beaufort must have come in extra early and brought Robyn with her. Seeing Jenny, Robyn stopped and ran over to talk.

"Hi," Robyn began. "So I hear Kat's trying to get you to help save the school."

Jenny blinked. "Save the school? From what?"

It was Robyn's turn to look surprised. "Didn't you know? My mom says Kat has this idea about putting on an original ballet and telling everyone you choreographed it. She thinks that might get enough publicity for the school that she can keep it open next year."

"You mean it might not stay open?"

"Well, not if Veronique gets into the National. Mom had thought of keeping it going if I was really keen on ballet, but I'd still rather do kung fu instead."

"Wait," said Jenny. "You mean if the school doesn't do this new ballet, your mom will close it?"

"No, no. It's like, the school doesn't really make enough money to stay open. The only reason it's been around so long is because my dad works for the city, which owns this building, so he got the city to give the school a big discount on rent. You know, supporting the arts and all. But if Veronique gets into National, my mom doesn't want to keep teaching. She'd rather move to Toronto to be with Veronique. Kat wants to keep the school going, but the city probably won't give her the discount. So unless enrolment goes up a lot, the school will probably close."

Jenny's brain was working hard to digest this news. "So, the ballet is supposed to get publicity, which will help enrolment, which will save the school?"

Robyn smiled. "Now you've got it. So is it true? Is Kat trying to get you to choreograph a ballet?" She said it as though she thought the idea was far-fetched.

"I'll tell you later," said Jenny, and she started walking very quickly toward the ballet school door. The school couldn't close. They couldn't take away Ara's chance to continue dancing, not after all the work she had done to get a solo. And what would happen to Lian's ambitions? Where would everyone else go, all the kids in the younger classes who wanted to learn more? Where would Jenny go?

The office door was open, and Jenny could see Kat sitting behind the desk chatting to Madame Beaufort, who was standing next to her. Jenny knocked on the door frame.

"Hi, Jenny," said Kat, smiling broadly.

"Can I talk to you for a minute?" Jenny asked, stepping into the office. "It's important."

"I'll leave you two alone," said Madame Beaufort. "See you this afternoon." She picked up a file folder and walked past Jenny on her way out.

Jenny stepped up to the desk determined to confront Kat. "Is it true the school might close next year?"

"Who told you that?" asked Kat.

"Robyn." Jenny didn't care at the moment whether it was a secret or not.

"Well, we honestly don't know yet what will happen next year. I hope the school will remain open, no matter what happens. I'm trying to find a way to make sure it does."

"Okay," said Jenny. But then she realized another question was forming in her mind. "Was that the real reason you asked me to do our ballet? Is it just for a publicity stunt?" She couldn't stop a hint of indignation from creeping into her voice.

"No," said Kat. "I asked because it deserves to be staged. Yes, I want to do something exciting for the recital, something that will show the community that this school is worth supporting and worth sending its children to, something that hasn't been done before. If I hadn't seen your DVD, I would have had to create something else. But I doubt I could have found a better opportunity."

"Really?" Jenny asked.

"Really. A ballet choreographed by a twelve-year-old, especially one with obvious artistic merit, is a pretty special thing. It's something that might attract media attention. But that's not the most important reason I'm asking you to do it."

Kat paused for a moment, as if considering whether to go on. Then she did. "Jenny, I feel as though this school failed you last term. We should have realized—I should have realized—what was going on and tried harder to help you.

"You have to understand ... sometimes parents send their children to ballet school not because the children want to learn to dance but because the parents like the idea. Often, we get mothers who took ballet when they were young or wished they had. Or maybe they just think their little girl will look cute in a tutu. Other parents don't have strong feelings at all. They just want their children to be involved in some supervised activity, so they give dance a try. I had a boy student once whose parents put him in ballet only because hockey was full. He was not very happy about it."

Jenny laughed. It made her think of Robyn.

Kat continued, "When you went to so much effort to avoid participating in class, I thought perhaps your parents were making you take ballet and that you didn't want to be here."

"I did want to," said Jenny.

"I know that now." Kat smiled. "When you showed up and asked to volunteer, I knew for certain that you must really have a love of dance. It was such an unusual request. It made me wish I had taken the time to get to know you sooner, maybe help you feel okay about participating."

"You couldn't have helped me," said Jenny. "Or maybe, just letting me watch was help enough."

"Well, at any rate, when I saw on the DVD how much you had accomplished on your own, how much natural talent and passion was waiting to be nurtured, I saw that you deserved—no—that you needed a chance to put that talent and passion to good use."

"But," Jenny began, "do you really think it's good?"

"I really do."

"And would it really be me choreographing, or you?"

"Well, there are things I can help you with, teach you. But I want this ballet to be as much your creation as possible—and not just as a publicity stunt—because you deserve the chance."

"Okay," Jenny said. "I'll do it. But I'm not sure about the actual rehearsals. I might just want to, you know, tell you my ideas and then watch from the sidelines."

Kat smiled. "That would be fine. We'll sit down and have a good chat about it all before we start. I'm glad you've decided to do it. Now, I see it's almost time for Pre-Ballet."

Jenny and Kat stood up and began walking toward the studio. "Oh, and by the way," Kat said softly, "I don't suppose there's any chance Ara has managed to keep this to herself? I forgot to ask you two to do that on Thursday."

"Um, probably not," Jenny said.

"Well, then, maybe I should poke my head into the Grade Four class today, just in case there are any questions. "

Chapter 23

A Tough Sell

That afternoon, Ara once again arrived extra early for ballet class. After kicking off her outdoor shoes at the door, she bounded over and sat down beside Jenny, who was finishing her lunch. "Hi! I wanted to see you before class," she explained. "I just had to know if you've decided whether you want to do our ballet."

"I do," Jenny said.

"Yes!" Ara exclaimed, bouncing up and down on the couch. "So what part do you want to be? I'd still like to play the swallow. Do you want to stick with the flower?"

"Whoa!" Jenny exclaimed. "I'm not dancing in it. In front of all those people? No way."

Ara stopped bouncing and sat up straight. "You're not going to be in it? After all the work we've done?"

"You should know me well enough by now."

"Well, okay. I guess someone else can play the flower. As long as I can be the swallow, I don't mind." Ara put her chin on her hands, grinning to herself. "I can't wait to see what everyone else comes up with for their solos."

"Um, what do you mean?" asked Jenny.

Ara looked Jenny in the eye. "Well, we're going to keep doing it the same way, aren't we? Improvising? Letting everyone have an important part? That's what's been great about it so far."

Jenny hadn't considered this. When it was just her and Ara, everything was simple. Two characters, two dancers, were all that could be on stage at a time. Ara was easy to work with because she could improvise to any piece of music and any idea Jenny could suggest. But there were close to sixty kids in the school. Jenny wasn't sure how they could have everyone improvising at once or how she could create a part for everyone. "Um, I'm not sure. I mean, I haven't thought about how to make it work with everyone."

"We have to keep doing it the same way," Ara insisted. "It can't be another recital like last year where only one person gets to stand out and everyone else just dances in unison. I don't want to be the star like Veronique was. I want to have a solo in a ballet where there are no small parts."

"You're right," Jenny said, realizing it herself for the first time. "We have to do it that way. But it's going to be hard." She paused and then put her hand on Ara's arm. "Can I ask you something?"

"Sure," said Ara.

"You know I'm scared. You know it's going to be hard for me."

"Yeah, I know. But I know you can do it."

"Okay, but I'm going to need help. I can't do it unless I know we're friends and you're going to help me."

"We are friends."

"I know, but can you promise me we'll stay friends, no matter what happens, even if I go all crazy and get upset about things that shouldn't matter? Promise me we'll stay friends at least until after the performance?"

"We'll be friends for longer than that. Friends for life. What do you say?" Ara shook Jenny's hand.

"Agreed," said Jenny. "For life."

Moments later, Trish walked in the door. "Hi," she said with a smile. She plopped down onto a chair and looked from Jenny to Ara. "So, what's the verdict?"

"We're doing it," said Ara.

"Cool."

"I told Trish about the ballet," Ara explained

"So when do we start working on it in class?" Trish asked.

Jenny was glad to see that Trish didn't think the idea was ridiculous or stupid. At least that was one person who might be on their side. "Um," said Jenny, "it's only just been decided. I really don't know. Kat said she'd be around to answer questions today."

"Well, it sounds like fun anyway."

As it turned out, everyone had questions about the project. In the girls' change room, Jenny had to say over and over that she didn't really know much about how this new ballet was going to be done. She couldn't avoid answering a few questions about the story, but she didn't really want to. She wished Kat was there and could talk to everyone for her.

When everyone assembled in the studio for class, Madame Beaufort clearly did not want to discuss the ballet either. Instead, she just let Kat tell the class that they would be discussing the year-end recital in detail in Monday's class and that everyone should hold onto their questions until then. She made no mention at all of Jenny or that Ara would be dancing a major role. Jenny thought this was just as well. The longer she could put off seeing Veronique's reaction, the better.

Jenny spent the rest of the weekend (after finishing her homework) trying to figure out how she could change the work she and Ara had done so far to give everyone in the school a big enough part to be noticed. She thought about how *The Nutcracker* worked, where the second act consisted of pairs of dancers taking turns to dance *pas de deux*. Of course, there were more boys in that company: older, stronger men who could lift the girls off their feet and twirl them around. Lawrence was the only boy in the Grade Four class, and Jenny had never seen him lift even one girl. She couldn't imagine asking him to lift each girl in the class over and over.

Then, of course, everyone in *The Nutcracker* had been a fully trained professional dancer. Jenny knew she could only ask people to dance the steps they knew.

Yet, the more Jenny thought about the story itself, the more possibilities she could see. There were places where the story could be expanded. Other characters could be brought in, other challenges created for the heroes. What she really needed was to sit down with Kat and see if there was a proper way to make the ballet fit the students rather than the other way round.

On Monday afternoon, Kat began class with a discussion of the ballet. "As you may have heard," she began, "we have a very special project in mind for our year-end recital this year. Jenny and Ara have been working on choreography for a new story ballet. I've looked at what they have done so far, and it's a very exciting and original work. So I have decided that the school should present it for our recital."

Veronique's hand was first in the air with a question. "Who's going to star in it? Them?" She indicated Jenny and Ara, who were sitting together. It wasn't a nice "them."

"Why don't I let Jenny answer that," said Kat. She gave Jenny an encouraging smile.

"Well," Jenny began. Her voice sounded small in the big space of the studio. "We haven't decided for sure. But I won't be dancing in it."

"Why not?" asked Trish.

"I don't want to. But Ara will have a big part."

"So you made your best friend the star?" said Veronique.

Jenny wasn't quite sure how to answer this accusation. "Well, Ara and I have been creating most everything together, so she knows it. But it's not like there's only one big part. We want to give everyone a chance to do something important, something to make them stand out."

"Guys," Ara broke in, "this is completely different from anything we've done before. The way we've been doing it on our own is that Jenny comes up with ideas and then we improvise around them, and then they get shaped into the final choreography. So that means you get to make your part what you want it to be, big or small, as long as it fits. We can all be stars." Ara looked at Veronique as she said her final words.

There were a lot of furrowed brows as well as excited murmurs as the class tried to picture this. Then Kristen raised her hand. "Why don't we just do something classical, like usual?"

Kat answered this one. "Classical repertoire is well worth knowing. But ballet isn't just about repeating works from the past. Real ballet companies are always developing new works that are relevant to today. Learning to take part in such a process is an important part of a dancer's training."

Lian's hand went up next. "Does this mean we're going to create a ballet that other people will see, not just our families?"

"Yes," said Kat. "If it goes according to plan, I want to sell tickets to the general public."

"Cool," Lian said.

Kat continued, "Actually, one of the reasons I chose to do this project is that I really want to help our school grow. I want it to be able next year to offer the best possible training and opportunities for all of you. That means we need the school to draw more attention and support from the community. And the way to do that is to give something of value to the community. So I want us to create something new, something wonderful, something surprising that will make people sit up and notice us."

"So, wait a second," said Robyn. "Does this mean that we'll have the chance to do whatever we like?"

"That's the idea," Ara said.

"As long as it fits in with the rest," Jenny added.

"So, can I do kung fu?"

"Um, I'm not sure," said Jenny, trying to picture in her head how kung fu fighting would fit into her ballet.

"Figures," said Robyn.

"Look," Ara butted in, "this is our chance to be like real artists. It's a chance to create whatever we want, the kind of ballet you always wanted to do."

Jenny looked at the faces around the room. Veronique and Robyn didn't look too happy, but the others seemed to be warming up to the idea. Maybe this was going to be okay.

Kat spoke next. "I'm sure everyone has a lot of questions as to how this is going to work. I'm not entirely certain myself. But I think that once we begin rehearsals, it will become clear. Right now, however, we need to get on with our class. Places at the barre, please."

Jenny sat down against the wall while everyone else got into position. Kat came over and whispered to her, "How would you feel about joining everyone for part of the class today?"

Jenny shook her head vehemently.

"All right," said Kat, smiling. "But can you stick around after class? We have some things to talk about."

The rest of that class proceeded as normal, except there was no improvisation. Instead, Kat made one more important announcement. "I want to say that you have all worked hard so far this year, and I feel you have developed the necessary strength. So, beginning two weeks from now, every class will devote a few minutes to pointe training. That's dancing on your toes. Of course, it's only the girls who dance en pointe." She looked at Lawrence. "Lawrence, I'm going to start you on some special training exercises. I want you to start developing your upper body strength at the same time the girls are doing pointe work. Meanwhile, girls, tell your parents that they need to buy you a pair of pointe shoes. Make sure you go to our recommended supplier and get properly fitted. Above all, I don't want to see anyone trying to dance in pointe shoes that are secondhand or ill fitting. You can ruin your feet. I'm serious about that. Okay, see you next week."

Jenny waited until the other students had left. "You wanted to see me?" she said to Kat.

"Yes, Jenny." Kat gathered the attendance sheet and other papers. "Let's go to the office for a minute."

Once in the office, Kat handed Jenny the DVD of her and Ara's rehearsal. "I made a copy of this. I hope you don't mind. I just didn't want to keep it in case you needed it."

"No," said Jenny. "That's okay."

"I wonder if you can do me a favour. Can you bring me the CD of the music you were using so I can hear it properly?"

"Sure," said Jenny. "It's all on one disc."

"Great. I just want to make sure we can get permission from whoever owns the copyright."

"Oh." Jenny hadn't thought about that. "Does it matter?"

"Oh, yes," said Kat. "We don't want to get into any trouble. Next, I want to ask you whether you have a system of recording your choreography."

"Um, not really. I made a lot of sketches. They're not completely organized because we've changed a lot. I sort of have the steps memorized. Plus, Ara pretty much knows what we've done so far."

"Well, I don't want to burden you too much. Dance notation can be pretty complicated to learn and use. But I do think you should have a way to keep track of your work. One simple way is to use the musical score. Do you read music?"

"Um, my dad taught me a little."

"Okay, good. So you can make a notebook with the musical score running along the top—or at least some way of knowing how many bars of music or how much time one page represents—and then underneath make a line for each dancer or group of dancers onstage and write down what each of them is doing at each point." Kat grabbed a notepad and pencil and made a quick sketch so Jenny could see what a sample page would look like. "Write in pencil so you can change it later. Obviously, it's easier if everyone is doing the same thing, or if there aren't too many groups to keep track of. Also, you can paste your sketches on the opposite page or make little diagrams showing where all the dancers are and where any props or set pieces will be. Just like little snapshots."

Jenny looked at the sketch and tried to imagine how much time one page would represent. "That's a lot of pages for a whole ballet," she said.

"You may need to get a big notebook," Kat admitted. "But I think if you give it a try, you'll find it will help you keep track of everything better. Start with the big picture—the broad movements. Then, think about how you're going to break those movements into phrases. Each phrase begins somewhere, explores something, and concludes. Try to vary the rhythm enough to make it interesting while still making sure everything fits together."

Kat must have realized this was a lot of information for Jenny to take in. "Don't worry," she said. "Those are really just pointers. You already know a lot of this instinctively. I can see it in your work. Just trust your instincts. We have plenty of time to fine-tune it as we go along."

"Okay," said Jenny. She didn't want to say that this looked like a lot more work than she had expected. But if this is what it took to make a proper ballet, she was willing to try.

Chapter 24

A Sneak Attack

On the way home, Jenny asked her father to stop at an office supply store and buy a thick binder, dividers, and a package of three-holed paper to make into a choreography book.

After dinner than evening, Jenny went to her room, put the paper into the binder, and labelled the dividers so there was one for each scene in the ballet. Then she grabbed the mystery CD she and Ara had been using for their ballet and went back downstairs.

Jenny's parents were sitting at the kitchen table. Her father was working on lesson plans, and her mother was doing paperwork she had brought home from the office. "Mom, Dad," said Jenny, "do you know what this CD is? I found it in the office. It's all piano music. I need to know who composed it because we're using it in the ballet."

Her father took it and looked it over. "I'm not sure. Let's listen to a bit of it. Maybe it will jog my memory." He carried the disc to the living room, put it into the CD player, and pressed play. After a few seconds, the music started.

From the direction of the kitchen, Jenny heard her mother cry out. A few seconds later, she ran into the living room. "Don't tell me that's the CD you want to use!"

"Yeah," said Jenny. "Why?"

Her mother looked at her father. "You remember this?"

He nodded. "Been a long time since I've heard you play it."

"What is it?" Jenny asked.

"This is a recording of music your mother and I wrote while we were in university," her father explained. "It started out as an assignment for a composition class. Then it got out of hand."

Jenny turned to her mother. "You mean that's you playing?"

"Yes," her mother replied. "Although, I couldn't play it nearly so well now."

Her father listened carefully for a moment. "You know, it's not bad. Sometimes, you look back on things you did when you were younger and they can seem amateurish. But this is okay."

"Well, we did get an A on it," her mother observed.

Jenny asked, "So how come you're not on this CD too, Dad?"

"Oh, I am," her father replied. "Didn't you notice that some of the tracks are duets?"

Jenny's smile widened. "Oh, yeah. I never thought about it before. Cool."

"Of course, I never could play anywhere near as well as your mom."

"Well, I guess we don't have to worry about copyright on this music," Jenny concluded happily. "I can use it, right?"

Jenny's parents looked at each other. Her father smiled. Her mother shrugged and said, "I suppose so. But make a copy of the CD first. I wouldn't want anything to happen to it."

"I can do it, hon." Her father got up and took the disc from Jenny. "Let's go up to the office."

Jenny suddenly got an idea. "Hey, does this mean you have the sheet music?"

Her father stopped to think. "Where would that be?"

"I think I know," said her mother. And she started to follow them to the stairs.

"Oh, and one more thing I almost forgot," said Jenny, turning back, one foot on the bottom step. "I need a pair of pointe shoes."

Both of Jenny's parents stopped dead in their tracks. "You need what?" asked her mother.

"Pointe shoes, for ballet school. Everyone in the class is starting pointe work soon." Jenny looked at her parents' puzzled faces. "What? I can't wear plain old ballet slippers if everyone else is wearing pointe shoes."

"Does this mean you've decided to start participating in class?" her father asked, hopeful.

"No!" said Jenny. "But I still need to dress the same as everyone else."

"Well, does it really make a difference? I mean, I understand those shoes can be expensive …"

"Dad! Of course it makes a difference." Jenny couldn't believe her parents didn't understand how important this was. "If I'm part of the ballet school, I have to dress like a dancer. Otherwise, I could be just anyone who wandered in off the street. And would they let someone who just wanders in off the street choreograph a ballet?"

"We'll talk about it later," said her mother, giving her father a quick glance as Jenny led the way upstairs, shaking her head.

Jenny's father photocopied the sheet music for her after making a duplicate CD. That night, Jenny cut up the pages and pasted the music onto three-hole paper—one line at the top of each page—and put the pages in her binder with dividers separating the scenes. Before bed, she looked through it one last time. The blank spaces on each page were crying out to be filled with life and movement. Her first ballet—it was very exciting.

On Wednesday, Jenny and Ara had their usual after-school practice. They spent part of the time reviewing their work on the ballet so far so Jenny could begin writing down the choreography. "After all," Jenny reasoned, "you've been playing almost all the roles so far, and you understand them. But I've got to be able to show Kat how the whole thing is supposed to look with everyone."

Ara looked at the binder Jenny had prepared. "I'm glad you're doing it and not me. I love dancing, but spending all that time thinking about it would drive me crazy."

That night, and for the next two, Jenny wrote in her binder, in pencil, an outline of the entire ballet as she envisioned it. As she worked, she kept coming up with new ideas that Ara and she hadn't tried out yet but seemed to fit. The idea of having more dancers to work with opened up many new possibilities.

At the same time, however, Jenny knew that a lot of what she wrote now would have to be changed. They had promised that everyone would have a chance to create their own parts, so Jenny couldn't get too specific about anything yet. She just wanted enough to show Kat that she was really making an effort.

Saturday morning, before Pre-Ballet, Jenny showed Kat her binder with all the notes she'd made so far. Kat promised she would read through it after the morning classes and give her some comments after the Grade Four class that afternoon.

Madame Beaufort, along with Robyn and Veronique, arrived shortly after the morning's classes had finished. The younger students had almost all left, and Jenny was eating an apple in the waiting room. The two girls sat down on one of the couches while their mother went into the office to see Kat. Veronique, Jenny noticed, was clutching a large notebook.

A few minutes later, Madame Beaufort stuck her head out of the office door and called, "Veronique! Come on in."

Veronique got up and went into the office, carrying her notebook.

"Well, I'll just leave you to it," said Madame Beaufort, and she left the office and went down to the studio. She smiled and said a quick hello to Jenny as she passed.

"What's going on?" Jenny asked Robyn.

"Trust me," said Robyn. "You don't want to know." Then, after a pause, she asked, "So, did you decide if there's any room in your ballet for some martial arts?"

"Actually," Jenny said, "I did have an idea for a fight scene."

Robyn's eyes widened. "Really?"

"Yeah," said Jenny. "You see, the ballet is all about this flower that wants to fly to the moon and gets this swallow to help her. I thought that, at one point, there could be this hawk who tries to attack the swallow and eat it."

"So, could I be the hawk?"

"Maybe. The thing is, the dancer playing the swallow wouldn't have to know martial arts because she's not a bird of prey. But the hawk could be, like, this great fighter."

"Could the hawk use White Crane style?" Robyn asked.

"What's that? Is it those arm movements I saw you doing in the corridor the other day?"

Robyn smiled. "No, that was *chi kung*. White Crane is a kung fu style where the moves are all, like, based on a crane's movements. You know, since a crane's a bird—"

"That would be awesome," said Jenny. "Do you know any? Can you show me?"

"I took a little last year. If we go into the hall, I can show you."

Jenny and Robyn got up and went to the hallway, where there was more space. Robyn launched herself into the White Crane solo routine, and Jenny immediately saw that Robyn's talents were being totally wasted in ballet. Dancing, Robyn always looked rather ungraceful and awkward compared to the others, but she executed the kung fu moves with an agility, speed, and poise that took Jenny totally by surprise. Robyn was one girl she never wanted to get into a serious fight with.

But what was even better, Jenny realized she had found the perfect hawk. "That's really cool," she told Robyn. "I think you should definitely play the hawk in the ballet and use some of those moves."

Robyn looked really pleased. "That would be great. My stepmom hates martial arts."

As the two girls began to walk back to the waiting room, Robyn asked, "Is there any way Veronique could be the swallow? I'd love to have a scene where I get to beat her up."

"Um, I think Ara's going to be the swallow."

"Oh, well, that's okay too."

Jenny was curious. "Why do you want to beat up your sister?"

"Stepsister," Robin corrected her. "Just wait until you find out what she's talking to Kat about. You'll want to beat her up too. In fact ..." A realization seemed to be dawning on Robyn's face. "You'd better talk to Kat right away, before Veronique ruins this great idea we've just had."

They reentered the waiting room just as Veronique and Kat appeared at the doorway to the office. Robyn flopped back onto the couch, leaving Jenny standing alone, wondering what she had meant. Jenny noticed Veronique was no longer holding her notebook.

"Well, leave it with me," Kat was saying. Veronique smirked at Jenny as she headed in the direction of the girls' change room. Watching her go, Kat shook her head. A rather annoyed look was on her face as she turned and went back into the office.

Jenny glanced at Robyn, who raised one eyebrow as if to say, "What did I tell you?" Jenny followed Kat into the office. "What was that about?" she asked Kat.

"That was a private conversation," Kat said sternly. Then her face softened. "But I suppose you'll find out soon enough."

Kat closed the door to the office so they could have some privacy. Then she pointed to Veronique's notebook, which was sitting on the desk. "Guess who has also come up with an idea for a ballet."

Jenny's jaw dropped. Then she felt a cacophony of feelings flood her mind and body: anger that Veronique would try to steal this opportunity from her, fear that she might succeed, unworthiness to compete with someone so talented, rejection. "Is it really good?" she asked, fearfully.

Kat sat down behind the desk. "From what she told me, I doubt it. It sounds like a loose amalgamation of two classical ballets, with some of the names changed." Kat picked up Veronique's notebook and leafed through it. "She has some very specific choreography written out ..." Kat scrutinized one page closely for a few seconds before continuing, "... which seems to have been plagiarized from the original. I suspect her mother helped her with this."

Kat was being unusually frank for a teacher, Jenny thought. Maybe it was because she was angry.

Kat skimmed through a few more pages silently. Finally, she said, "I'm pretty sure Veronique simply wants to be in the spotlight, so she's trying to undermine you by putting forward her own idea. Maybe she thinks I'll change my mind and let her choreograph instead." Kat continued to flip pages as she thought. "The thing is, it probably would make things easier if we used some part of what she's done, even if we changed it in rehearsals or cut it later."

"It's okay," Jenny said. "I understand if you'd rather do her ballet. I know Madame Beaufort probably wants it that way."

Kat raised her eyes and looked Jenny in the eye. "Not a chance," she said. "I had to argue long and hard with her and the board to get them to agree to producing your ballet, and I'm not backing down now. This school will do an original work this spring, and that's that."

Jenny suddenly wished she had spent longer on her binder. She hoped it was good enough to justify Kat's efforts on her behalf.

Kat thought for another moment and then said, "How about I give this notebook to you for the weekend? Skim through it. You may find some of the terminology hard to follow—the parts that were copied, that is. But see if there are any ideas in it you think you could use. Something to make Veronique feel she made a contribution. Only, whatever you do, don't let anyone else know I gave it to you. Just keep it in your bag until you get home."

"I'll have to get my dance bag," Jenny said. She opened the door, dashed out to the waiting room, grabbed her bag, and dashed back. She took Veronique's notebook from Kat and stuffed it in her bag. It barely fit.

"Oh, by the way," Jenny said, "would it be all right if we had a kung fu fight scene in the ballet? I sort of promised Robyn, and I have an idea of how it could work."

"It's a little unorthodox," Kat said, "but as long as it fits what you're trying to express."

"Oh, it does," Jenny assured her.

"Well, then, you're the choreographer."

Jenny started to turn around to leave, but Kat said, "Wait. Since you're here, we should talk a little bit about Monday."

Jenny turned back. Kat continued. "What we will need to do is start using part of each class to rehearse or develop sections of the ballet. Since Monday is the first day, we could simply start by telling everyone what the story is about. That might be easiest."

"Okay," Jenny said.

"Also, could I ask you to hold off telling people what roles they'll have, at least until you run it by me? There are a few things I'd like you to take into account before making any final decisions. Besides, you should leave some room for flexibility. You may discover things in rehearsal you don't know yet."

"Okay," said Jenny.

Kat put a hand on Jenny's binder, which was still sitting on the desk. "I'd like a little more time to study what you've done, but so far this looks very promising. If you come a few minutes early on Monday, I can talk to you more about it.

"After Monday, I'll be taking on more of Madame Beaufort's

classes, and it would be helpful if you could come to some of them too—as long as your parents don't mind."

"Okay," Jenny said again.

"Don't be nervous. I'm going to help you as much as you need. If you want me to run the rehearsals and you just make comments afterward, that's fine. If you want to run the rehearsal and have me watch and just intervene if necessary, that's also fine."

"Okay," Jenny said for the fourth time. There wasn't much else she could say. The thought of working with so many students was overwhelming.

"Oh, and let me give you my home phone number." Kat took a business card out of a desk drawer, wrote on the back, and handed it to Jenny. "I don't give this out to everyone. Otherwise, I'd get too many phone calls from parents in the evening, when I'd rather they just left a message with the school's answering service. But if you have an emergency when I'm not here, I'm giving you permission to call me—just not before nine a.m., especially on Sundays."

Just as Jenny was turning to go, a thought occurred to her. "Um, Kat?"

"Yes?"

"If I'm here most days from now on, Ara and I won't have time to practise together."

"Well, I'd like it if Ara can be at more classes too. The two of you have accomplished a lot together, but it would be better if you could do your work together here so I can help you more. If you want, you can use the studio for a few minutes each day before classes start."

"Okay, I'll ask her."

That night, Jenny read through Veronique's notebook in bed. It was written neatly, using a number of professional-sounding terms, some of which Jenny didn't understand. But she could see why Kat thought it had been copied from other ballets. The story didn't quite make sense. And for some reason, all the scenes involved one dancer doing a long solo routine while all the other dancers either sat and watched or did little chorus-y things at the beginning or end. Jenny hated the idea of putting any of these scenes into her ballet.

Then Jenny had an idea. Maybe all it would take to satisfy Veronique and Madame Beaufort would be one scene where Veronique had a chance to shine. Surely, Jenny could find a part for Veronique in her ballet that would let her have her moment. A glimmer of an idea started to occur to her. Maybe there was such a part. But it wouldn't be a straight solo. Oh, no. Jenny would make Veronique dance with everyone else, not in front of them. A delicious feeling of satisfaction flowed through Jenny as she fell asleep imagining what the scene would look like.

Chapter 25

Brainstorming

On Sunday morning, Jenny started to think seriously about the first rehearsal of her ballet, which would take place the following day. Or, more precisely, she began to worry about it. She knew what she wanted to do, which was to plunge right into the kind of practice Ara and she usually had. But the thought of doing it with everyone there set her heart racing. In the end, she realized there was only one person she could turn to for help, and that was Ara.

"Help!" Jenny shouted into the phone when Ara answered. "I'm incredibly nervous about tomorrow. You've been in recitals before. You have to tell me what to do."

"It's exciting, isn't it?" said Ara. *Exciting* was not the word Jenny would have chosen. "But don't worry. It will be fun."

"How? I don't know what to do. What do I do?"

"You just do what the teacher says."

"I'm the teacher! Or at least I'm the choreographer. I don't even know what a choreographer does."

"Hmm," said Ara. "I've never really thought about what the

person in charge does. Usually, she just gives us sequences of steps, and we practise them in class until we have them memorized."

"But I don't have all the steps worked out. What do you do when you're using improvisation?"

"We've never done a recital based on improvisation," Ara said, "but I guess you could put the music on and tell that part of the story, like when it was just you and me. Give people parts. And everyone could improvise. Hey, maybe you could use your camcorder to record the improvisation and then use the recording to write down the stuff that worked? Then, next time, we could just rehearse what you've decided on."

Jenny thought about this. "That kind of makes sense. I suppose we could just start with the first piece of music. By the way, did I tell you my mom and dad wrote that music?"

"No, really?"

"Yeah, way back before I was born. Then they totally forgot about it."

By the time Jenny got off the phone, she felt a little calmer. She still didn't really know what to expect, but at least she felt she could make a plan.

Jenny took the bus after school on Monday to make sure she arrived early for ballet. After putting on her dance outfit in the empty change room, she found Kat in the studio, in the process of sticking long strips of masking tape onto the floor. "Hi, Jenny," Kat said, straightening up. "I've just been laying out the floor plan for the stage. You've never seen this done, have you?"

"No," said Jenny.

"Well, the area I've marked is exactly the same size as the stage in the theatre we'll be using," Kat explained, pointing to various strips of tape. "I've marked the locations of the side curtains. The audience is toward this side of the room. This helps us see where dancers can enter and exit the stage and exactly the number of steps required to get to various positions. That way, the choreography won't have to be adjusted when we get to the theatre."

"Kat," said Jenny, "are you sure I can do this? There's so much to know about ballet, and I hardly know anything."

"Yes, Jenny. I believe you can. You don't have to know everything. I'm here to fill in the blanks. All I want you to focus on is doing what you do well—imagining and shaping ideas."

Jenny pulled Veronique's notebook out of her dance bag and handed it to Kat. "I read this. I don't want to use any of it, but I did get an idea that might make Veronique happy."

"Good," said Kat. "I read your binder too. Let me give it back to you." She led the way over to the piano, set the tape down, picked up Jenny's binder, and handed it to her. "You've made an excellent start. I wrote some suggestions for you—just questions, really, that I'd like you to think about before we start rehearsing those sections—and a few places where some of the enchainments we've worked on this year might fit. Have you thought about what you'd like to do today?"

"Well, I did have a couple of ideas," said Jenny.

The first half of the class was much like any other. Jenny continued taking notes on everything and drawing sketches in her notebook. The only difference was that now she was looking at each exercise as a source of ideas she could use in the ballet.

Toward the end of the class, Kat invited Jenny to come and join the other students. Jenny walked over to where Ara stood and then sat on the floor with her binder, facing the rest of the class. Sitting felt safer than standing, especially when everyone else sat down too. This was the closest Jenny had ever come to participating in the class, and she felt strange and nervous. Ara's face, on the other hand, bore a look of excited anticipation.

"Um," Jenny began, looking at the floor. "Well, as you know, Ara and I have this idea for a ballet."

"A little louder, please, Jenny," said Kat, encouragingly.

Jenny looked up and tried again. "Ara and I have this idea for a ballet. But the thing is, it's not quite finished. And besides, we want it to be not just our ballet but something everyone can contribute to. So I thought, before we start, I would ask for ideas. What sorts of things would everyone like to have in the ballet?"

"What do you mean?" asked Kristen.

"Well," Jenny continued, "like, if you could imagine the perfect ballet story or if you could put anything you like in a ballet, what would you choose?"

Trish looked at Kat. "We've never done this before. Is this allowed?"

"Absolutely," said Kat.

"Kung fu," suggested Robyn.

"Got that," said Jenny. She started a list of ideas on a blank page in her binder.

"Designer costumes," said Trish.

"That may be limited by our budget," Kat pointed out.

"What else?" asked Jenny.

"A love story," said Ara. This brought a few smiles and a few quick glances at Lawrence, who was the obvious candidate for a male romantic lead.

"Adventure," suggested Lian, "like travelling to some exotic, far-off place."

"A happy ending," said Kristen.

"A princess," said Veronique.

"Monsters and fight scenes," said Lawrence.

As the ideas kept coming, Jenny wrote them down.

"Fairies."

"Mermaids."

"Aliens."

"Magic."

"How about a scene where they have to swing on a rope, like in a pirate movie?"

"How about a pirate ship?"

"What about a scene where someone has to die to save her friend?"

"A wedding."

"A funeral."

"Someone who starts out a nobody and becomes great."

The ideas kept coming, and Jenny filled one page and started a second.

"Can we do all this in one ballet?" asked Kristen.

"Um, I don't know," said Jenny. "But we can try." She looked at the list. It was getting very long. "Maybe for now, though, we could listen to some of the music we have for it?"

Jenny pulled the CD out of her dance bag. She walked over to the CD player and put the disc in. The first track was a piece that Ara knew well.

"This is the part where the flower first wakes up," said Ara. She then explained to the class, "There's this flower that wants to visit the moon and gets a swallow to help her. Want to see?"

A few heads nodded, so Ara stood up, went to the centre of the floor, and began to dance the part of the flower. This was a dance Jenny usually did when it was just her and Ara, but she was quite happy to let Ara do it today. Of course, Ara couldn't resist changing a few things, but that was okay for now.

There was a change in the music. "Okay," said Ara. "Here's where the swallow enters. Jenny, you want to be the flower now?"

Jenny shook her head. "No, you show them."

"Okay," Ara continued, "so pretend the flower is still here, and now this swallow enters." And Ara began to dance the swallow's part.

Jenny was glad to have Ara taking the spotlight for the moment. If anyone else had done such a demonstration, Jenny thought, it would look like showing off. But with Ara, somehow you knew she was just trying to make some of her own enthusiasm rub off on the group. It seemed to work too. When the class ended, there was a lot of excited discussion as the students filed out the door.

Before Jenny and Ara left, Kat pulled them aside and said, "Well done. You won some support today, and that will be a big help later on."

Chapter 26

Rehearsals Begin

When Jenny opened her binder that evening, she found that Kat had stuck in several sheets of comments. Since much of the ballet was not clearly worked out yet, Kat's suggestions were pretty general. But she did have some useful tips, such as using all of the stage (including each of the four corners), varying the rhythm and height of movements, and making connections between the beginnings and ends of scenes. She had written out for Jenny a list of what steps students in various grades and classes had learned and could be asked to perform and pointed out that Jenny needed to assign each class a particular scene or role they would dance together. She also said that Jenny shouldn't make the ballet too long.

Remember, Kat concluded, *if you get stuck or if it seems too much, let me know. I can help fill in any missing bits.*

Jenny appreciated the offer, but there was also a part of her that wanted to do it all herself.

Next, Jenny turned to the list of suggestions everyone had made in class. Some of the ideas would be easy to incorporate into the existing story. Others would be harder, but maybe with a little thought ...

At eleven p.m., Jenny snuck downstairs to make an emergency call to Kat. She had been lying awake thinking about an idea and didn't think she could sleep until she had an answer. Kat had told her not to call before 9 a.m. on Sundays, and this was certainly later than that, so Jenny hoped she wouldn't mind.

"I'm sorry to bother you," Jenny whispered into the phone, hoping her parents wouldn't hear, "but is there any way we can get some skateboards? Ones with a big surface on top? I had an idea of how to put mermaids in the ballet."

There was a long pause. "Just make a list of things you think you want," Kat said patiently. "If they fall within our budget, I'll try to oblige."

"Thanks," said Jenny.

On Tuesday, Jenny had her first real rehearsal with the Grade Two Ballet class. She had decided that the Grade Twos were to dance the part of the moon creatures to a very ethereal track on the no-longer-a-mystery CD.

Jenny was glad this class was first. She was a couple of years older than the students in this class, which made them less scary to talk to. Yet, at the same time, they were old enough to do steps that were far beyond those the Pre-Ballet students could do.

Toward the end of the class, Kat introduced Jenny and explained that she would be helping them with this year's recital. Jenny put the music on, and Kat invited the students to improvise being moon creatures who lived in a low-gravity environment.

As the students improvised, Jenny made sketches of movements she liked and made suggestions to Kat, who then conveyed them to the students. When the class ended, Jenny had a number of ideas she felt could be incorporated into the ballet.

For the next two weeks, Jenny used a similar approach in every class. Kat would reserve a certain amount of class time for improvisations having to do with *The Moonflower and the Swallow*, and Jenny would use this time to experiment with ideas.

At first, Jenny let Kat do most of the talking to the class. But gradually, she realized it was easier to make suggestions herself. Just like when she was working with Ara, Jenny would arrive with an idea for part of the ballet and then let the class improvise to the music while she called out additional ideas or instructions. One day, Jenny realized to her surprise that she had led the entire improv session herself while Kat just looked on.

Ara came to most of these classes as well. She and Jenny did warm-ups together before classes started. Ara would then dance the swallow part when it was needed and help whenever Jenny felt the class needed a demonstration.

Jenny found it challenging to keep up with her homework with all these extra classes, and her mother kept reminding her of her promise. But Jenny found she could get a lot done during recesses and lunch hours at school.

Because Jenny was wearing her dance outfit every day, it grew smelly quickly. So her dad found time early on to take Jenny to the dance supply store and buy her two new leotards, three pairs of tights, and a pair of pointe shoes. At first, Kat hadn't been keen on letting Jenny wear pointe shoes to rehearsals, but Jenny had pleaded vehemently and in the end Kat relented, on the condition that Jenny was not to stand, walk, or dance en pointe for any reason unless Kat gave her permission.

After the second week, the dances gradually became more fixed. As they did, Jenny recorded them in her binder after class. Sometimes, she would video the classes to help her remember later. Kat offered many suggestions on how to improve the choreography, some of which Jenny agreed with and some of which she didn't. Kat never forced her to change anything. But sometimes, after thinking about it, Jenny would decide Kat was right. Other times, Jenny would find a different solution to a dance that still took Kat's suggestions into account.

Jenny followed Kat's advice in assigning each class a separate scene in the ballet. This made things easy since each scene could be rehearsed in the appropriate class. "Of course," Kat explained, "once we get close to the performance dates, we will need to have a few rehearsals that involve the whole school."

Jenny assigned all the characters that appeared more than once in the ballet to students in the Grade Four class. At first, this bothered her. She had hoped to give every dancer an equal part, but it just wasn't possible. Besides, the Grade Four class had learned more and could do more, so it made sense to reward them with more stage time. And, as Kat explained, the kids in the Pre-Ballet and Beginning Ballet classes were so young that they had a hard time remembering their choreography. They needed to dance in unison so they could see what their neighbours were doing whenever they felt unsure of the next step.

However, when it came to the Grades Two and Three students, Jenny deliberately avoided having them dance in unison. She tried to give each dancer her own individual routine, her own journey to take in the story. She wanted every dancer to have a moment when she stood out.

All of this took a tremendous amount of time and effort. Jenny's choreographic work took up all her evenings at home, in addition to her time at the ballet school. But she found nothing pleased and excited her more than seeing the ballet get better with practice.

In fact, all things considered, these weeks were some of the happiest Jenny had ever known. She was doing something she truly loved. She had found a place where she felt accepted and appreciated. Her friendship with Ara was stronger than ever. Everything, in fact, went remarkably smoothly until the arrival of the skateboards.

Chapter 27

Mermaids

Jenny had had the idea of casting Veronique in the role of a mermaid princess whose people were endangered by pirates who were harpooning merpeople for sport. With the help of the swallow and her friend the flower, whom she carried on her adventure, the pirate captain fell in love with the mermaid princess, and peace was established in the oceans. It was one of several adventures the swallow and the flower had on their way to the moon.

Jenny's idea was to have the dancers playing mermaids lie on their backs or sides or stomachs on skateboards. With scenery to block the audience's view of the wheels, they could dance while balanced on the skateboards and it would look like they were actually swimming in the ocean.

Most of the mermaids would be played by the Grade Two class, with the Grade Fours playing the pirates. Jenny wanted Lawrence to play the pirate captain and Veronique to play the mermaid princess. Their wedding *pas de deux*, Jenny thought, would give Veronique her chance in the spotlight.

The skateboards arrived one Thursday in time for the Grade

Four class. Unfortunately, when Jenny tried to explain her ideas, Veronique was less than happy.

"I am not dancing on that! No, no, no."

"But see, the idea is to look like you're actually swimming," Jenny argued, pointing at Ara, who had borrowed someone else's skateboard and was whooshing across the floor, banging into everyone in turn. For some reason, she had chosen to play this game wearing her pointe shoes.

"That is not ballet," Veronique insisted. "I didn't spend all this time learning to dance en pointe just so I can roll across the floor like a five-year-old on a waterslide."

"But I think it will look really cool."

"And what happens if someone, like her—" Veronique pointed at Ara, "rolls off the stage and crashes into the orchestra pit? Or knocks someone else off stage?"

"Well, it might take a bit of practice."

"Face it." Veronique was literally looking down her nose at Jenny. "You don't know what you're doing. And she—" Veronique pointed at Ara, "should not be dancing a major role."

At this point, Kat (who had been running over some sequences with a few of the girls but still overheard all this) began walking over to Veronique and Jenny.

Veronique saw her coming and spoke first. "Miss Miles, I can't do this. What good is a recital if I can't do what I'm good at? I'm a dancer. I use my legs. Who's going to see what I can do if I'm sitting on the floor on this thing? And besides," she turned back to Jenny, "how am I supposed to dance a *pas de deux* if I have a fishtail? My feet will be stuck together!"

"Well, I thought you could be carried in on a platter ..." Jenny began.

"Ahhhh!" Veronique screamed. "This is so stupid!"

"Okay, Veronique," said Kat. "Let's just calm down."

"Ow," came Kristen's voice. Kat and Jenny turned around to see Kristen shaking her finger. Apparently, Ara had just run over it with her skateboard.

"And that—" Veronique pointed at Ara and spoke loudly enough for the whole studio to hear, "is why she should not be a principal! Between her stupid antics and—" Veronique now pointed at Jenny, "her stupid choreography, this whole school is being ruined."

Now Ara was angry. She stood up and marched up to Veronique. Jenny thought for a second Ara was going to hit her. She wondered if Robyn had taught her stepsister any kung fu moves. But then Ara stopped, looked Veronique pointedly in the eye, struck a perfect arabesque, and executed a *tour de promenade*—a slow turn on one foot, en pointe. It was a very difficult move, which no one in the class had yet learned. As far as Jenny knew, this was the first time Ara had tried it. It was her way of saying, "So there!"

Kat was horrified and rushed over to Ara to make sure she hadn't hurt herself doing an advanced step she wasn't ready for and wasn't supposed to know.

Veronique's mouth dropped open in astonishment. Her face flushed with humiliation. Before anyone could say another word, she grabbed her bag and stormed out of the studio.

Since there were only a few minutes of class time left, Kat suggested it might be better if they finished a little early. Veronique had already left the girls' change room by the time the skateboards had been put away and the rest of the class went to change for home. Everyone was unusually quiet.

Finally, Ara said, "So, does anyone else think my antics mean I shouldn't be a principal?"

Kristen, who was trying to button her shirt without using her sore finger, gave Ara a look that suggested she might agree with Veronique. No one else said a word.

"I didn't want to be like a star or anything," Ara continued. "I just wanted all of us to have more of a chance. I thought if I had the spotlight, I could make room in it for everyone else. That's why we're doing the ballet this way."

"Don't worry about Veronique," said Trish. "She just doesn't want to be pushed out. It was a pretty cool turn you did."

"Thanks," said Ara. "I think I hurt my toe a little, and maybe my ankle, but it was worth it."

Robyn looked at Jenny. "Don't worry about what she said about the choreography. The less it looks like ballet, the better, as far as I'm concerned."

Jenny didn't find that comment the least bit comforting. She was starting to feel that the skateboards—an idea she had been excited about—were a mistake. Maybe she didn't know what she was doing. Maybe Veronique was right.

Jenny wanted to talk to Kat before she left about what had happened in class. When she had changed and went to the office to find her, however, she could hear Kat and Madame Beaufort's voices through the door. She wondered if Veronique was there too.

"How long are you going to allow this sort of chaos to continue before you intervene?" Madame Beaufort was saying. "Jenny is just too young and inexperienced to do the job you've given her."

There was a long silence in which Jenny's heart fell. If Kat wasn't fighting back, that meant that maybe she agreed with Madame Beaufort. Jenny listened intently. She had to know what Kat really thought.

"Not every experiment works out," Kat finally said. "This is just part of the creative process."

"But our parents don't pay for their children to be involved in experiments. They want to see ballet, as they expect it to be. You think you have a couple of dances that are working. Fine. Keep those and fill out the rest of the recital with something a little less ambitious."

"I'd like to try to avoid that," said Kat. "It wouldn't be a ballet then, just a showcase."

"That's what a recital is. That's all anyone expects."

"I know. That's why I won't do it unless I absolutely have to."

At supper that night, Jenny's mother asked her, "What's wrong? You've hardly eaten anything. You usually come home ravenous after a rehearsal."

"Did it not go well?" her father asked.

"No," said Jenny. "Veronique doesn't like the choreography. Madame Beaufort thinks it's my fault." She paused. "Even Kat's thinking of replacing it."

Her parents exchanged glances. Then her mother said, "You know, Jenny, your father and I were talking the other night. Ever since you and Ara started getting together, you've been working so hard, such long hours. It's too much. I don't remember the last time you watched a TV show, or read a book, or did anything that wasn't ballet. It's too much for a girl your age."

Jenny could see there was some truth in what her mother was

saying. She hadn't watched TV since Christmas. And she did miss having a little free time. "I thought you wanted me to do something productive?"

"Yes, but not every hour of the day. I don't know how you've managed to keep up with your schoolwork."

"I have, though."

"Yes, and that's great. But I'm just afraid this may be too stressful for you."

Jenny realized then where this conversation was going. "But I love ballet," she insisted. "The only thing that's really stressful is the thought of not doing it."

Her mother continued. "I know you've really enjoyed having Ara as a friend. But aren't there girls at school you could be friends with too? Girls with other interests?"

"I don't like the girls at school. All they ever talk about is clothes and pop music and boys. They never talk about anything interesting. Most of them never even read books."

"Have you given them a chance?"

Jenny could feel her whole body tensing up. She couldn't take any more of this conversation. "Can I go now?"

Her mother sighed. "All right."

After Jenny stomped up the stairs, her mother said, "I just worry that this ballet thing has given her unrealistic expectations for herself. It's so much responsibility at her age!"

"Well, maybe we can speak to Katrina," her father offered. "She seems like a reasonable person. Maybe there's a way to lighten Jenny's load."

"I think I should speak to Ara's parents too," said her mother. "Maybe they have some of the same concerns."

Chapter 28

Persistence

When Jenny reached the top of the stairs, she went straight to her father's office to phone Ara. "I've made a decision," she said after they exchanged hellos. "I don't want to give up on the ballet."

"Great," said Ara. "I don't either. But what do we do about Veronique?"

"I have an idea," said Jenny. "Could you ask your mom if you can come to the dance school a littler earlier tomorrow, maybe right after school?"

"Probably. Why?"

"I want to try something."

There was a spare room in the building that housed the Kingston Ballet School. Any of the tenants that rented premises were allowed to use it on special occasions. Jenny knew the dance school sometimes held fund-raising events or meetings there. Most of the time, though, the room was empty. When Jenny met Ara at the dance school the next day, she asked Kat if she could borrow the key to this room.

"What do you plan on doing?" Kat asked.

"Fixing the mermaid scene," Jenny answered.

Kat gave Jenny the key, and she and Ara walked down the hall and unlocked the door. For some reason, only half of the room was carpeted. The floor of the other half was covered in shiny linoleum tiles. A large table sat in the centre of the room. Along one wall were several stacks of chairs. Each stack rested on a square, wooden rack with casters on the bottom. The racks allowed the chairs to be easily rolled to wherever they were needed.

"I saw someone from one of the offices borrowing these chairs last week," Jenny explained to Ara. "Help me take the chairs off one of the racks."

"Why?" Ara asked.

"You'll see."

The two girls removed chairs from the stack, one at a time, until the wooden rack was empty. Jenny put one foot on the rack and tried pushing it in different directions. "What do you think?" she asked Ara.

Ara tried. "It turns easier and sharper than the skateboards. It's wider, so it will be easier to stay on. But I think it might move too easily."

"I'm guessing it will be easier to control with someone's weight on it," said Jenny. "And Kat told me they always mop the stage with cola before a ballet to make it less slippery."

"So you think we can use these instead of skateboards?"

"Why don't we try it?"

For the next hour, they experimented with the chair rack. As Jenny had suspected, it was easier to control than a skateboard. Ara tried different ways of lying and dancing on it with her upper body in the air, or her legs, or both sets of limbs. Jenny also had her practise different ways of propelling herself across the floor, turning, spinning, and stopping.

In the end, Ara was exhausted. But by then, Jenny knew exactly how the mermaids should move.

Ara waited in the spare room while Jenny ran back to the dance school to ask Kat if they could borrow the chair racks for the last half hour of the Grade Two Ballet class. When she came back with permission, Ara and Jenny took the stacks of chairs off their racks, piled the empty racks on top of each other, and began pushing the jiggling pile down the hall toward the school.

"Well, this is okay," said Ara, "but how are you going to get Veronique to do the mermaid dance?"

"I have another idea for her," said Jenny. "I think she'll like it better."

That night, Jenny rewrote Veronique's part again and again in her binder until the paper was nearly worn through from erasures. There was only so much music and a lot of story to tell, but in the end, she thought she had something that would work. On Saturday morning, she showed it to Kat.

"It's a neat solution," Kat said. "It may be a bit complex, especially in terms of scenery and effects, so you may need to pare down a few other scenes. But let's try it. Well done. Now the next question is, will your cast go for it?"

"... so then the pirate captain sees the mermaid princess, who's sunning herself on a rock. He falls instantly in love with her and invites her on board. She thinks he's cute and calls the other mermaids, who help her into a giant magic clamshell. The pirates haul the clamshell onto their ship, and when she emerges she has legs instead of a tail, so the *pas de deux* and the wedding are then done on the deck of the pirate ship. But then, the swallow warns the mermaid princess that the pirates are planning to kill the other mermaids and take their bodies as trophies, so the princess dives overboard to warn them. But just after she does so, one of the pirates throws a harpoon into her and she dies." Jenny looked up from her notes into the faces of the Grade Four class. "At least, I tried to fit everyone's ideas in, and this is the best way I could think of."

Jenny turned to Veronique "I worked out a way that includes all your best moves. You'll be like the Sugar Plum Fairy in *The Nutcracker.* You won't have the most time on stage, but your dance will be the most spectacular. You can do the *pas de deux* on two legs, standing up, as well as a mermaid dance on the rock, and a death scene, with no skateboard."

"I think it sounds really cool," said Trish.

"Me too," said Lian.

Most of the other heads were nodding in agreement. Jenny waited to see how Veronique would react.

"It's a good story," Veronique admitted. "I like the tragic death."

"So," Kat asked, "does everyone agree that this ballet is worthy of being staged?" Everyone nodded.

"I have to tell you," Kat continued, "this is an ambitious production for a small school like ours. To pull it off successfully will require not just hard work but commitment. Jenny and Ara have worked very hard to bring the ballet to this point. From now on, we all must be willing to put the ballet ahead of any personal conflicts. You all have to work together as friends. If you do, and you make the ballet something that touches the hearts of your audience, it will be an experience you will remember for the rest of your lives. So what do you say? Is everyone willing to try?"

A chorus of yeses filled the room. Jenny paid close attention. Even Robyn had chimed in.

On the way to the girls' change room that day, Veronique pulled Jenny aside. "I'm sorry I called your choreography stupid," she said. "I think the new version is really cool. No one ever choreographed a dance especially for me before. I can't wait to rehearse it." Veronique smiled a big smile.

Jenny was so surprised. "Thanks" was all she could think to say. But she felt amazingly happy for the rest of the day.

For the next several weeks, rehearsals went very smoothly. Every student seemed to be trying her (or his) very best to learn the parts. Veronique worked hard on her portrayal of the mermaid princess and even came up with a few ideas of her own, which Jenny was happy to include. The mermaid princess even spent some time en pointe, at which Veronique was ahead of everyone in the school, with the possible exception of Ara.

For the longest time, Jenny tried to have Ara rehearse all of her sequences that involved pointe work when Veronique was not around to avoid fuelling any rivalry between them. Veronique's abilities had continued to improve, thanks in part to ongoing private lessons with Kat, but Ara had come far as well. After Ara's demonstration on one foot, Kat had made a special effort to coach Ara on improving her pointe technique. The two girls were now practically equals in their technical ability.

Ara, however, surpassed Veronique in passion. As much as she tried to restrain herself and focus on control, Ara brought an emotional quality to her performance as the swallow that always took Jenny's breath away.

As the performance date approached, Kat recruited many parents to help with aspects of the ballet. Some built set pieces and props, and others sewed costumes. Lian's father designed and printed posters.

One Monday, two reporters, a photographer, and a cameraman arrived at the studio to talk to everyone and film some of the rehearsal. Kat had invited them to do feature articles on the school, the upcoming ballet, and Jenny for the local newspaper and television station. Jenny was quite nervous having her picture taken. When the reporter asked her questions, her brain seemed to freeze up and her mouth seemed to be capable of one-word answers only. Fortunately, Lian was nearby. Seeing Jenny's difficulty, Lian jumped in and began explaining in great detail what the ballet was about, how Jenny was choreographing it, and how exciting it was to be doing something new and original. Then the cameraman filmed a little of the rehearsal, while Jenny tried her hardest to stay out of camera-shot and forget he was there.

That night, Jenny had to leave the living room when the story about her ballet came on the evening TV news. She felt too embarrassed to watch it, but her father recorded it. And when the article was printed in the newspaper a few days later, her mother clipped it and posted it on the refrigerator.

Chapter 29

Performance

Kat decided the ballet would have its opening night on the last Friday evening in May. There would be two more performances on Saturday, including an afternoon matinee, and a final matinee on Sunday. Kat explained to Jenny that that was the most they could ask from the youngest dancers and their parents. Parents and other relatives of the dancers generally bought enough tickets to fill one performance. The rest were a gamble. But the publicity had helped advance ticket sales, and Kat had made a special arrangement with the theatre that if the Saturday shows were poorly attended, they could cancel Sunday.

The Wednesday and Thursday before, rehearsals were held in the theatre. This was an old building, built over a hundred years ago before movies became common, but it had recently been refurbished. The dressing rooms still smelled of new paint and carpeting.

At this stage, there wasn't much Jenny needed to do. All the choreography had been firmly set days ago, so Kat ran the final rehearsals. She knew all the tips to give everyone about how to behave backstage, how to make an entrance, and what to do if anything went wrong. She also knew how to coordinate with the technicians who were in charge of lighting and sound and the parents who were dropping off, picking up, and dressing their kids.

For most of the Wednesday and Thursday evening rehearsals, Jenny stayed in the stage left wing. She had volunteered to be on hand just in case anything needed doing there. As things turned out, her only real task was to help the Pre-Ballet students get ready for their entrance. The darkness in the wings was a little scary for them, so Jenny would go to the greenroom a little bit ahead of time, where all the kids waited, line them up, and lead them through the crossover, hand in hand, to the stage left wing. Once there, she got them ready for their entrance and sent them onstage at the right moment. The rest of the time, she sat in the wing and watched the ballet.

Jenny was a little nervous about stepping onto the stage itself, even though it was just a rehearsal. The theatre was such a huge space. The stage felt so much bigger than the studio, although Kat assured her it was the same size. Maybe it was because the ceiling reached up several stories, or because the wings on each side made it look bigger, or because one side was open to the "house," where the audience would sit on hundreds of seats that stretched all the way to the top of the balcony. Whatever the reason, Jenny felt more comfortable behind the curtains, trying to pretend the house didn't exist.

On opening night, Jenny had her parents drive her to the theatre early—so early, in fact, that she was the first one there, apart from the theatre staff, so her parents stayed with her until Kat arrived.

In the Grade Four dressing room, Jenny changed into an all-black outfit in order to work backstage. Even though she was not performing, she still felt she had to dress like a dancer. But Kat had convinced her to wear black tights and ballet slippers instead of her usual pink ones. Black, she had explained, was the traditional colour for the stage crew because it helped them appear less visible when changing scenery. Not that Jenny was expected to do that job. Lian's and Kristen's fathers had volunteered to move the pirate ship and other set pieces on and off stage, and most of the other scenic effects were being done with lighting.

There was a small props table in Jenny's wing, where a few extra props were stored. These included a fake harpoon, the tip of which had been made from one of Ara's old foam batons, and a foam-and-wire flower. This was a small replica of Lian in her flower costume since Lian was dancing the flower part. She did a beautiful job of it, but after the first scene, the swallow (Ara) had to carry the flower in her beak. So they had set up this cool effect where Lian would disappear slowly through a trap door (which had an elevator under it) while Ara bent down over her, concealing her exit with her wings. Then the lights would fade out, and Ara would run into the wing of the theatre and grab the foam flower from the props table. When she went back onstage for the next scene with the flower in her mouth, the audience would understand that the swallow had plucked the flower and was taking it with her on her journey.

Of course, when the swallow finally reached the moon, Lian traded places with the foam flower once again so she could dance the part of the flower, but in the meantime, much of the ballet revolved around what happened to the foam flower. For instance, in the second scene of the ballet, the flower was stolen from the swallow by a gang of mischievous fairies, played by the Grade One Ballet class. Jenny had choreographed the entire scene around the idea of these fairies passing the flower from one to the other, until finally the swallow was able to take it back.

In fact, the flower was such a key part of the ballet that Kat had made two foam flowers, just in case one became damaged partway through a performance.

As students began arriving, Jenny tried to make herself as useful as possible, mainly to take her mind off her nervousness. Kat had appointed one of the parent volunteers to sign dancers in, while other parents helped girls with their hair and costumes. Jenny helped wherever she could and checked every costume, prop, and piece of scenery several times, even though there was really no need.

Ten minutes before showtime, Jenny stood in the wings, listening to the murmur of audience members finding their seats, her throat very dry and her stomach very jittery. When the music began to play over the sound system, indicating that the ballet would start momentarily, Ara came over to Jenny and gave her a hug for luck. "Have a great performance," Jenny told her.

Finally, Kat made the rounds, asking everyone to get into their places. Jenny decided to stay in the wing, even though there was nothing for her to do there for some time. She just had to see the start of her ballet.

Seconds before the curtain went up, Ara turned and whispered to Jenny, "Oh, by the way, I had a great idea. Instead of running offstage after the first scene, I'm going to stay onstage. That way, I can strike this pose—," she demonstrated it, "and be in exactly the right position when the lights come up. Should be easier, eh?" Then she ran to her starting position.

No! Jenny wanted to shout. *Don't change anything now.* But it was too late. The curtain began to rise. The lights came up, and the music for the first scene began. Onstage, in the centre of a white spotlight, Lian begin her opening dance as the flower.

Jenny's eyes darted back and forth from Lian to the audience. She could just see the front few rows on the left-hand side of the house. They didn't look like they hated the ballet—yet, anyway.

Then Ara danced onto the stage. Her splendid navy blue and white costume, carefully highlighted with sequins, glittered in the stage lights, and she moved with an energy and grace that took Jenny's breath away. She was the swallow, in spirit as well as body.

Jenny tore her eyes away from the stage for a moment. She thought she might check on the Pre-Ballet girls, even though they still had plenty of time. Her eyes fell on the foam flower sitting on the props table. *The flower.*

Ara had said she was going to remain onstage after this scene. If she did, how would she pick up the flower? If she didn't pick up the flower, the rest of the ballet would make no sense.

Jenny's heart began to race. There was no way to get a message to Ara now. Would she remember the flower in time? Maybe not. She had so much else to think about, after all. So what could be done? Someone would have to give the flower to her. Jenny looked around the wing. No one else was there, except for a stage technician who was dressed in blue jeans and a T-shirt with a rock band logo on it. There was no way he could go onstage and look like he was part of the show. Every other person who was dressed like a dancer was either in the greenroom or in the other wing of the stage waiting for their first entrance.

Was there time to run through the crossover to the other side wing, grab someone—anyone who was dressed in a dance outfit— and get her to take the flower to Ara? Jenny looked onto the stage to see what part of the dance Ara and Lian had reached. No, it was too late in the routine.

What could she do? Jenny dashed to the props table and grabbed the flower. Maybe she could throw it to Ara. But that would look stupid. Why would the flower be sailing through the air if the swallow was supposed to be standing beside it? And what if she missed and the flower landed in the wrong place? Or stabbed Ara in the eye?

The dance was nearing the end. Ara was standing over Lian. The elevator began taking Lian down.

And suddenly, Jenny knew what she had to do. She had no other choice.

Jenny took a deep breath, and as the lights faded out, she ran across the stage to where Ara stood.

Jenny came to a halt next to Ara in the darkness and held out the foam flower. Just then the lights came up. Jenny realized she was now standing onstage under the bright lights, in front of the entire audience. She also knew that whatever she did now, it had to look like it was part of the ballet.

Just take the flower, Jenny thought desperately.

Ara's face showed a brief flicker of surprise at seeing Jenny standing there. Then a trace of a smile played on the corners of her mouth. But instead of taking the flower, Ara drew back in pretend fear.

Oh, my God, Jenny thought. *She wants to improvise.*

Sure enough, Ara began circling around Jenny, who still held the flower out to her. There was no music because what they were doing was not supposed to be in the ballet, so the theatre was deathly quiet. Jenny forced herself to focus on Ara to the exclusion of everything else. Ara lunged toward her, and Jenny instinctively stepped back. *I get it,* Jenny thought. *I'm a blackbird who snatched the flower from the swallow at the last second.*

Jenny began to copy Ara's bird-like movements, circling Ara on *demi-pointe* just as Ara circled her. It was a bit like the mirror improvisation they had done so long ago. But as they each began to give and take from each other, the dance began to assume its own form. It became a conflict between two birds, a fight over who would get to keep the flower. Finally, Jenny saw her chance to escape. In a moment of decision, she eluded Ara and executed a series of leaps to take herself offstage as quickly as possible. Ara followed, like one bird chasing another.

In the wing, Ara grabbed the flower from Jenny, whispered, "Good for you," and dashed back onstage, holding the flower triumphantly, ready for what was supposed to be the second scene.

Jenny grabbed hold of Trish, who had been standing in the wing watching. Jenny's knees buckled underneath her, and for a second she thought she was going to collapse onto the floor.

"Are you okay?" said Trish, as she helped Jenny into a chair that was sitting against the theatre wall.

"Yes," said Jenny.

"I was a bit worried Ara wouldn't have her flower," Trish continued. "There was so much to do to get ready. I'm glad you thought of a way to get it to her. Nice bit of choreography. When did you guys rehearse that?"

"Um, I'll tell you later," said Jenny, breathing hard. She was feeling light-headed and in no state to explain that the ballet had nearly been ruined, that all their hard work could have been wasted, all because of yet another one of Ara's crazy impulses.

After a few minutes of slow, deep breathing, Jenny remembered that she had to check on the Pre-Ballet students. She made her way slowly to the greenroom. The girls were ready and waiting for her. "Okay, let's go," she said, and she led them slowly over to the stage left wing.

When the curtain came down on the final scene of the ballet, Jenny was still in the wing, listening intently. Apart from Ara's mistake at the beginning, everyone had danced their very best. So if the ballet totally bombed at this point, it would be all Jenny's fault.

After a three-second pause that felt like eternity, the house exploded in applause. When the curtain rose once more, the entire audience was on its feet. Jenny knew that 75 percent of them were probably parents and grandparents of dancers in the cast, so they pretty much had to applaud. But they wouldn't have stood up if they had hated it. Jenny found that she had tears running down her face.

As the applause died down, Kat stepped onto the stage, bouquets of flowers cradled in one arm and a microphone in her opposite hand. She gestured to Ara, who had just completed her final *reverence*, to meet her down centre.

Kat handed Ara the bouquet and gave her a small hug. Ara whispered something in Kat's ear, and Kat handed her the microphone.

Ara smiled at the audience and spoke. "I just wanted to say that everyone who danced in the ballet tonight did such a tremendous job. We're all stars tonight. And also, I wanted to say a special thanks to the biggest star of all, who almost never made it on stage but who choreographed the whole ballet—our most unexpected dancer, Jenny Spark." All the dancers on stage turned and looked to where Jenny stood in the wings. They gestured for her to come out onto the stage.

Jenny's knees were buckling again, but she wiped the moisture off her face, took a deep breath, and walked out to where Kat and Ara stood. She faced the audience, and in traditional ballet style, did a *grande reverence* to the audience. Then she started to waver. Luckily, Veronique and Trish quickly stepped forward and put their arms around Jenny to steady her.

Chapter 30

What Happened?

Jenny sat in the greenroom, hunched over, with a bouquet of roses in her lap. She thought Kat had given them to her but wasn't sure. In fact, everything that had happened in the last few minutes was a bit fuzzy. She wasn't even sure how she'd gotten off stage. But the trembling in her legs had stopped, she was breathing normally, and to her surprise, she realized she was really happy.

Just then, she heard the sound of voices and the thundering of many feet on their way to join her.

"You know, I never thought I would actually enjoy ballet, but this show has been a blast," Robyn was saying as she and Trish walked into the room.

"I know," said Trish. "I was worried I wouldn't get the timing down for that final dance, but somehow tonight it just fell into place. Hi, Jenny."

Lian practically ran into the room a second later. "Hey, I don't know if anybody cares, but apparently there was a reviewer from *The Globe* here tonight, sitting in the front row."

Trish, Robyn, and Lian flopped down on one of the big couches, continuing to talk about the show. Other dancers arrived, dressed in their white moonflower costumes. Jenny stayed quiet, even when a minute or two later Kristen sat down beside her and spoke. "You know, I think I've decided what I want to do with my life. I want to work in a theatre."

"You mean as a dancer?" Jenny asked.

"No. I think I want to be one of the people running the show—stage manager or something like that."

"Cool," said Jenny.

"Hey, Jenny!" came a voice from the hall. One of the Grade Two dancers stuck her head in the door. "Your mom and dad are here!"

Jenny got up and went out to meet them. Her father had a bouquet of flowers in his hand.

"Congratulations, sweetie," her mother said, giving her a hug. "You did an incredible job. I'm sorry if I ever doubted you."

Jenny looked into her mother's eyes and saw that there was real emotion in them. "Thanks," she said.

"And congratulations on finally dancing," said her father, handing Jenny the flowers and giving her a hug of his own. "Nice leaps."

"Thanks," said Jenny. "But, actually, I wasn't supposed to be on stage at all. Ara forgot she had to get the flower, and I had to get it to her. Otherwise, it would have ruined the show."

"Well, it looked great, whatever the reason."

"Thanks," Jenny said again. At that moment, she realized that, despite all her fear and anxiety at the time, when she had danced across the stage, it had actually, deep down, felt wonderful.

Jenny sniffed her flowers. She looked at her parents, smiling proudly at her, and remembered the sound of the applause. And it suddenly occurred to her, for the first time, that maybe ballet wasn't just something she felt a longing for. Maybe it was something she could actually do.

The greenroom was getting crowded now as parents and children were busy searching for each other and reuniting. Jenny realized she wanted to change clothes before helping get the costumes and things organized for tomorrow, so she excused herself and made her way to the dressing room she shared with the Grade Four class.

Ara was the only person in the dressing room when Jenny arrived. She was just hanging up her costume on the rack. "Hi," Ara said. "Wasn't that a great performance tonight? I'm so happy for you! What finally made you decide to dance? Did you plan it all along as a surprise, or was it just a sudden urge? I thought it went pretty well considering we never even had one rehearsal!"

"Ara!" Jenny was flabbergasted and angry. "It's your fault I had to go on stage. I didn't want to. When you changed your choreography at the last minute, you forgot you had to go offstage to get the flower. I had to bring it to you, or else it would have wrecked everything."

"What do you mean?" Ara asked. "I asked Trish to hide the flower onstage—inside that fake rock right beside the trap door. I was planning to pick it up when the lights went out and no one would see. But then you came onstage with the other one, so ..."

"Oh my God," said Jenny in a small voice. "So I didn't have to go out there, onstage, and dance in front of hundreds of people, after all." She sat down in the nearest chair.

"You thought I forgot?" said Ara.

"I'm sorry." Jenny felt slightly dizzy. She looked into Ara's eyes. "I guess I should know by now that I can always count on you, at least when it's something important."

Ara sat down in the chair next to Jenny. "I guess I know I can always count on you to watch my back."

Jenny looked at her. "You can, you know."

"I know."

Jenny changed into her jeans, T-shirt, and street shoes and hung her black leotard, tights, and slippers on the costume rack. Then she went to help tidy up the costumes in the large dressing room that the younger students were using. Luckily, there were enough mothers helping as well, so it didn't take long.

Finally, Jenny decided to take one quick look at the stage before she left. The props and scenery hadn't been moved since the performance ended. Jenny spent a few minutes putting things in place for tomorrow's performance. Then she walked onto the stage and looked out over the empty chairs. It was maybe a little less scary now.

As she turned to go, Jenny's eyes fell on the artificial rock. She walked over to it and looked inside. There was no flower hidden there. Trish must have forgotten to set it in place after Ara asked her.

Chapter 31

New Directions

The three remaining performances went off successfully as planned. Kat thought the dance of the swallow and the blackbird was worth including in every performance. She found some appropriate music to cover it, a shawl that helped Jenny's arms look like wings, and a black cap to affix over Jenny's dirty-blonde hair.

Jenny was reluctant at first, but she decided in the end that even if something went wrong with the dance, Ara could probably improvise a way out of it. Ara, naturally, insisted that there was no turning back. Jenny was a dancer now, and she owed it to herself to stay a part of the ballet. However, Jenny did insist that they rehearse the new dance a few times on Saturday morning, before the next performance.

On Sunday afternoon, the curtain came down for the last time on the Kingston Ballet School's production of *The Moonflower and the Swallow*. It was a sad but also happy event. Everyone said it was the best recital the school had ever put on. Cleaning up took a little longer because all the costumes and props had to be packed away, the set dismantled, and the dressing rooms emptied. After that was done, all the students and their parents were invited to share refreshments in the greenroom as Kat and Madame Beaufort took the opportunity to hold a short meeting.

Madame Beaufort had two important announcements. First, Veronique had received her letter of acceptance and would be attending the National Ballet School's summer program and, with luck, the fall semester as well. She was the first student from the Kingston Ballet School to advance to bigger opportunities in the world of dance.

Jenny, Ara, and Veronique were all sitting together eating cake. Both Jenny and Ara whispered their congratulations to the new graduate.

"Thanks," Veronique replied. "I think working on the mermaid princess role really helped me with the final audition."

Madame Beaufort's second announcement was that she was resigning from the school. "I have loved teaching these past four years. But it's time I handed the job onto someone better qualified than I. I hope you will give your full support to our school's new artistic director, Katrina Miles."

There was a round of applause as everyone expressed their appreciation for Madame Beaufort and welcomed Kat.

"Thank you, Madame Beaufort. I know your work at the school will be deeply missed," Kat began. "Especially since, thanks to the publicity surrounding this year's ballet and its success this weekend, the school has had a lot of new people asking about classes for next year. In addition, we have received a very generous amount of donations, so thank you to everyone who contributed.

"The upshot of all this is that our school will be able to expand. So, over the summer, I will be conducting a search for new staff and possibly looking to add to our studio space as well." This brought a buzz of excited whispers throughout the room.

"I want to say that I am particularly proud of what we accomplished this year. This is the first time this school has staged an original story ballet. I wish I could take credit for it. But as I hope you know, it's really the result of two extremely talented girls—one of whom, Ara, was our prima ballerina, and Jenny Spark, who choreographed the ballet. We are very lucky Jenny was so determined to be a part of the school that when she couldn't take classes, she became a volunteer and then exceeded all expectations by proving herself to be a gifted choreographer."

Again, there was another round of applause for Ara and Jenny.

Kat continued. "I also want to say that this was a very risky production. It was risky in terms of its financial cost. It was risky because we asked a lot of your children. And it was risky because nothing like it had been done before in this city. But I want to say that I have always believed that for ballet to play an important role in a community, to make a valued contribution, it requires a certain amount of risk. Not too much," Kat glanced at one of the board members, "but a little. You should be very proud of your children. And I hope we will be able to do equally exciting productions in the future."

After the meeting and refreshments were over, the students and their parents began to leave. This was the last time many of them would see each other until next fall, when ballet classes began again, so the good-byes took longer than usual.

Just as Veronique and Robyn were going out the door with Madame Beaufort and her husband (whose last name, Jenny had learned, was Miller—same as Robyn's), Ara stopped them. "Remember, Veronique, you promised us postcards!"

"I'm sorry," said Veronique. "I mean, I'll write to you."

"Will you be back next year?" Jenny asked Robyn.

"I'm not sure." She looked at her parents. "Only if I can't do kung fu."

"She'll be back," said Mr. Miller.

As soon as they had waved good-bye, Jenny and Ara turned to see Kat coming toward them. "Can you girls come with me for a moment? There's something I want to speak to you about."

Kat led the girls to one of the now empty dressing rooms. On the way, she collected Jenny's and Ara's parents. "Have a seat, everyone," she invited.

Kat chose a chair for herself as well. "I just wanted a quick word before you all left. I want to ask whether Jenny and Ara will be returning next year to take Grade Five Ballet?"

Ara's parents looked at each other uncertainly.

"That is, would you like Jenny and Ara to take ballet if there were no financial impediments?"

"Yes!" Ara said right away.

"I want to," said Jenny.

"Good. You see, it has been the practice of the school in past years to award a scholarship to the most improved student of the past year. I'm happy to say that with strong ticket sales and new donations, I can offer scholarships to two students for next year. You two have certainly shown more improvement in one year than I would have thought possible."

Ara looked at each of her parents in turn. Finally, Mr. Reyes nodded. Mrs. Reyes turned to Kat and said, "Yes, Ara will definitely be coming back next year."

"That's excellent. However, Ara, before I grant you this scholarship, there is something I need to hear from you."

"What's that?" Ara asked.

"I understand that on opening night, you decided to change your choreography."

"Yes. That's when I had the idea of saving a trip to the wing …"

"And that decision nearly caused a minor disaster, didn't it?"

"Yes," Ara admitted. "But that's what got Jenny dancing, and we created that new dance with the blackbird, which you said was good—"

"I know what I said," Kat interrupted. "But I want to make sure you understand how reckless your actions were. What if things had gone differently? You know how much work everyone put into the ballet? You know how many people in the audience paid good money to see the best performance we could give them?"

"Yes." This was the first time Jenny had ever seen Ara look sheepish.

"A dancer can't afford to take selfish risks, not when others are counting on you to do your part as rehearsed. We're just lucky Jenny was there to help you out."

"I'm sorry," Ara said.

"That's what I wanted to hear. If you want this scholarship, I expect you to set an example to the younger students in the school of what is proper behaviour for a principal dancer."

"I will. That is, I'll try my best."

"Very well."

Ara turned to Jenny and said quietly, "Dance class is going to be very different next year, isn't it?"

"Yes," said Kat. "I think it will be. Now, Jenny." Kat turned to scrutinize her. "What am I going to expect from you next year?"

Jenny lowered her eyes for a moment and then looked back at Kat. "I guess things can't go on exactly the way they have, can they?"

"No," said Kat, "they can't. Jenny, you're a mystery. A girl of your age, with little formal dance training but an amazing talent for choreography. A dance student who won't participate in classes but will improvise in front of a live audience. What can I say? The scholarship is yours if you're going to use it. But from now on I want you participating in class. You can't avoid it anymore. I know you can dance!"

Kat pointed her finger in such a display of mock exasperation that Jenny had to laugh. "I've actually been thinking a lot about it," Jenny said. "I think when I started dance classes last September, I wanted to dance so badly that I couldn't get past being afraid I'd be no good at it."

"And now you know you can dance?" asked Kat.

"No, now I don't want it so badly."

"You're not quitting ballet!" Ara exclaimed, horrified.

"No." Jenny laughed. "I don't mean I've stopped wanting to dance. I mean, I'm not so afraid of it. I think what I really want to do now is choreography."

"Do you want it so much that you won't be able to do it?" Ara asked, teasingly.

Kat threw her head back. "Oh, great. I gain a dancer but lose a choreographer. Is that it?"

Jenny laughed again. "I hope not. But I think that in September, I'd like to take dance lessons. I mean, actually take them, not just watch. I have learned so much this year." Then she pointed her finger jokingly at Kat and said, "Don't try to stop me!" Everyone laughed.

"Mr. and Mrs. Spark," said Kat, "does Jenny have your permission to accept this scholarship and take ballet lessons again for the first time in September?"

Jenny's father looked at her mother. "You certainly can't object now. What better sign could you ask for?"

"You're right," her mother admitted. "Jenny deserves to continue with ballet. But I still have two conditions I want met."

Jenny rolled her eyes. "I know, make friends and keep up with schoolwork. I did, you know. Or at least I will, after I finish my geography project that's due tomorrow that I just remembered."

Jenny's mother shook her head but let this revelation pass without comment, for the moment.

"Good," said Kat. "Then I'll look forward to seeing you in class as well. You have a bright future, Jenny."

"Oh, I don't know about that," said Jenny.

"That's it!" Kat rose to her feet. "Out, both of you! See you in September."

Kat said good-bye to Jenny's and Ara's parents. Jenny and Ara ran to their dressing room and picked up their dance bags. Then they collected their parents and left the theatre for what was hardly the last time.

The End

About the Author

Glen C. Strathy started writing stories when he was 11 years old and became enamored of the arts and the opportunities for self-expression they offer people of all ages and backgrounds. Coauthor of a New York Times Bestselling Business Book, he has also worked as an actor, teacher, and freelance writer. *Dancing on the Inside* marks his fiction debut.

Glen graduated from the Artist in Community Education program at Queen's University, Kingston and earned his M.A. in English from the University of Western Ontario. His website www.how-to-write-a-book-now.com provides advice to budding authors.

CPSIA information can be obtained at www.ICGtesting.com
Printed in the USA
LVOW111646290312

275322LV00011B/25/P